The Way Out

First published in 2024 by
Adazzle Press

www.adazzlepress.com

First printing
1 3 5 7 9 10 8 6 4 2

ISBN (paperback): 979-8-9899672-0-9
ISBN (ebook): 979-8-9899672-1-6

Book designed and typeset by InsideStudio26.com

THE

WAY

NATASHA BURGE

OUT

Adazzle

60 Days

I walk on into the souq, into the crowded press of bodies, into the women in their abayas and the men in their thobes and the children in their sandals, shrieking their wayward shrieks. All around me the hot night shakes with the call to prayer, as the men in the mosque courtyard wash their feet – slick fingers spray out from between curled toes, while a wide shadow gathers on the ground below. At the edge of the street is Green Jack on his corner, speaking about the end of it all, and from across the highway comes the dark inky scent of the sea.

On past the street of silversmiths and on past the street of hotels, past the antiques shops with their wooden wares jumbled like sleeping beasts on the pavement. I turn the corner and pass the electronics shops, whose TV-filled walls blaze violence into the night, and pass the row of cobblers caught in their cloudy scents of leather and rawhide. Twinkling Diwali lights blink on as I turn another corner, painting the sidewalks with puddles of gleam. I hear snatches of conversation in Tagalog, Malayalam, Urdu, and Arabic. A listing wooden sign that reads: *The Best Gold Deals in the Arabian Gulf* is so weather-beaten, so faded with time, that the finely painted lettering is almost illegible. Jewelry stores shine with local pearls, karak cafés billow out steaming wafts of saffron and scalded milk, and music stores selling Egyptian oud and darbouka next to stacks of American tapes and CDs leak tendrils of music into the night.

Up ahead, two men shout, arguing. A woman leans out of a third-floor window and drops a scarlet shawl to a friend below. It slow spirals in the humid air like a fish caught in a lazy current. The waiting friend dashes forward and catches it. The two men have stopped shouting and they watch in silence as the woman wraps the shawl around her neck and up over the crown of her head. And then we all watch as she winds her way down the street, hips rolling in the murky dark.

At Shockwave Electronics I find two clerks carrying a giant clock into the shop window. Their faces twist with the effort. In the unseasonable heat, they are both sweating, and damp patches darken the backs of their shirts. When they reach a tall white podium in the center of the window display, they pause, make eye contact, and heave. Arms straining, they lift the clock into position. A sign above them reads: *Countdown till the End* in jagged yellow lettering. The words are supposed to look like lightning bolts. Next, they bring out a long digital display and slide it onto a shelf behind the clock. It blinks in red letters: *60 Days till Y2K! The End is Near!* Seeing this I realize that every day the minute hand of the giant clock will tick down to signify one day closer to apocalypse.

The men take stock of what they have done, wiping sweat from their foreheads, and then notice a fine crack in the giant clock's casing. Examining it for a moment, they mutter to one another, and then shrug and climb out of the window display. With the men gone, the glow of the digital display bathes the clock in red light.

At the end of this street is the white archway of the Madkhal building, curving over the main boulevard leading into the souq. And beyond the Madkhal's cool calcium eye is the sea. I cross to the other side of the road, keeping my head down, avoiding the alley that opens onto a view of the water. I walk fast past a falafel shop and a smoking shawarma spit, and then turn at the intersection, not letting the water make itself known to me.

But walking so quickly, turning so quickly, has done something to my body. A twist of nausea twines through me in a way that makes me think I am about to vomit, right here and now on the side of the street. A grim-faced woman pushing a stroller gives me a wide berth. I watch her baby as they pass, the small plastic face of it making me think it might not even be real. A shopkeeper spots me and leans out of his shop waving a glitzy shawl spangled in the stars and stripes of the American flag. Speaking English, he quotes me an outrageous price, and I realize he thinks I'm a tourist, that I have not lived all my life on these streets.

I realize, too, I am in pain. The accident happened days ago, but to my body it is still happening now. Within me, the hurt crackles, making me think of the lettering on the poster at Shockwave Electronics, as if I am filling with lightning bolts that limn in sulfur yellow those places that days ago made first impact with the street – my knee, my hip, my head. Earlier, in a bathroom sink, I spat out a long ribbon of blood; coiled on the white porcelain, it was a word I could not read.

I watch a tour guide and his flock of tourists approach an archeological site that is wedged between a cold store full of sodas and cigarettes, and a silversmith. While the tour guide talks, the tourists nod studiously, peering at the dirt lot marked off with a wooden fence, their faces red and shiny with sunburn.

'This land,' the guide says, 'has been continually inhabited for thousands of years. There were the Achaemenids, the Assyrians, the Babylonians, on and on into the past.'

The guide's voice carries above the squall of traffic, and people on the street turn to look. 'Waves of people,' he continues, making a watery motion with his arms, 'waves and waves of them.'

One of the tourists lifts his camera and all of the eyes on the dark street are blinded by the flash.

In the emergency room a few days ago, right after the accident, a nurse asked if my pulse was always so fast. Her face was creased with shadow beneath the glare of the fluorescent lights. 'Is your pulse always this fast?' she repeated, her hands moving across my body like small animals.

I told her I didn't know, which seemed wrong. To not know something about one's body, to be unaware of the secret measures it keeps, felt irresponsible, as if I had been neglecting some fundamental duty.

Standing now at the corner, watching the tour guide give his speech, it feels like there is a heart beating in my mouth. Punching at the base of my teeth, fast and then faster. I lift a hand to my throat. Carefully, as if I may find something I will not like, I search for the stretch of skin that conceals my carotid artery. Pushing with my finger, I find the leaping. It is so close to the surface, this portion of the body that carries so much, one disaster and all would be revealed. I push harder, I feel the moving thread, and I wonder.

Then, in the slender space between two beats, I see him.

An impossible man, his face a crack in the order of things. Wild radiance of hair, wide slash of a mouth. The crowd, dense with its heated motions, closes in and he disappears.

My hand drops from my neck. I wait for the crowd to dissolve so I can see again the impossibility. First to emerge is a young woman with eyes ringed in blue shadow. She looks up and down the road; she does not know where she is. Next is an old man with a mustache dyed so black it looks like a gaping hole at the center of his face. Then, bursting free from the center of the multitude, comes a trio of children with painted faces – this one a knight in armor, this one a violet butterfly, this one a frog with bulging eyes.

And then him.

Closer.

His fingers are as fine and white as fish bone.

The world tangles and I tell myself not to run.

He is passing directly in front of me, his head swiveling in my direction. When he finds my face, he looks at me like we know one another and, just as I know they will, his eyes catch the light and spin like stars.

59 Days

I stand naked in front of my bathroom mirror, my tools laid out gleaming. I've gathered what I can: tweezers, a metal nail file, scissors, and an oyster knife that I found in a drawer of the kitchen when I moved in. In the weak light of the bathroom's single bulb, they look sharp and very cold.

When I woke in the emergency room after the accident, I was not surprised: my mother had always made sure that I knew bodies were sites of catastrophe. While I had been briefly unconscious, tests were performed, and as soon as I was lucid Dr Ashguf, his yellow mustache disguising a mouth that may or may not have existed, told me I was fine. He said it was a miracle.

There could be lingering symptoms, though. He told me this was common with concussions. Disturbances, he called them. Headaches, nausea, dizziness. They might last weeks.

Which was why, when last night I saw in the space between two heartbeats an impossibility, Al Ghareeb – The Stranger of the long ago – I knew he was not real. It did not matter that he looked at me like he recognized me, or that his eyes spun exactly as I had always said they did. He was not real because he could not be real. He was a disturbance, a byproduct of my brain having been smashed against my skull, and so I let him go.

When I left the ER, Dr Ashguf had pleaded with me to take better care of myself. Over his mustache his eyes were heavy with concern and he kept using the word 'trauma', drawing out the middle vowels and waving them around like a flag. While he spoke, I twisted the plastic ER bracelet so tightly around my wrist that my hand went numb, filling with silver static.

Assessing my reflection now in the mirror, I feel like I've stumbled into a situation in which I don't belong. My eyes look wary and I see that the purple bruise running along the side of my face has taken on the shape of a hand. It spreads across my jaw and mouth as if someone has been trying to suffocate me. I probe tentatively behind my ear, and my fingers emerge dark and tacky with the remnants of old blood.

The grit begins in the weeping stretch of road rash that runs from my right hip down my thigh, over my knee, and along my calf. The nurses had wanted to remove it in the emergency room, coming at me with face masks and flashing instruments, but I had kicked them away.

I try now to remove it myself. From my tools I select the nail file, deciding something long will work best. I manage to pry a few of the larger pieces free, but the edge of the file is too thick to get under the more deeply embedded bits of debris, so I leave it aside and pick up the tweezers. Their sharp corners work perfectly and soon I am moving quickly down my sore skin, setting free whatever I find.

Along the outer rim of my knee there is a particularly deep laceration that sends quakes of pain through my body at the slightest touch. I've found an exposed wire within myself, something electric and sparking. I probe at what looks like a shard of glass with the tweezers. Wiggling it back and forth in the pulpy tissue of my flesh, my face flushes hot and my eyes begin to water. Gritting my teeth, I plunge deep into the wound, digging and digging, heart racing, breath whistling in and out of my nostrils. Everything exists here now, between the striations of red, pink, and white.

As she works, slowly digging out bits of gravel from raw crevices of torn skin, she feels like she is watching the process from a great distance, like she might be someone else. She dislodges bits of asphalt, pieces of glass, and a single strand of green thread. Sometimes, as she plucks at the pieces, they fall to the floor, but other times they soar through the air to click against the mirror or drop into the sink.

When she is finally done, she takes stock of her reflection. Thin streamers of blood run toward her feet, bright and new. The length of her right leg is gruesome but the grit is gone. She worries about infection taking hold in the wounds, about impurities finding their way into the secret passageways of the body.

In the mirror, the reflection buckles. The restless mouth, the ugly spill of hair – she looks, for a moment, like Al Ghareeb. Then she notices that her clavicles are uneven: the right one sweeps higher than the left, like it wants to leave her body behind. Lifting a finger, she presses on the sharp edge of the bone, pushing at it, wondering if it is higher than it was yesterday. Yes, she thinks, yes. She is different than she was.

58 Days

Asfara Avenue is full of bodies. There are too many eyes and scrabbling hands and I can smell the wet armpits and dirty tongues. I push my way into the mob and know that I smell no better. I think I showered yesterday. Or maybe it was the day before. I remember blood on my fingertips and fuzzing beneath my long toenails, but the memories are out of order, staggered in a way that makes me dizzy to think of them for too long. There is nothing that makes sense and all around me the night thrums on in this vibrating season of heat and doom.

I walk by the narrow mouth of a dark alley, catching the tail end of a low whisper slinking like a cat from the shadows. And then a real cat, flesh and bone and fleas, limps around the corner, ribs vaulting from her skin like leaping fish. On past a row of shops: Future Cold Store, Spider Cold Store, Sun Day Cold Store, and Shop Today Cold Store. Inside, they are all the same, lights blinking over cathedrals of crisps, candy bars, coolers of soda and juice, shelves of laundry detergent, and cartons of cigarettes. Behind the counters slump tired men who are busy missing distant families in distant countries.

With a throaty growl a sports car slices through the street, and the crowd falls away to either side. The boy at the wheel is wearing his gutra cobra-style in crisp crenellations of white around his young face. This used to be the street where all the embassies were. Now, it's halwa confectioners, tailors, and clothing stores. Disassembled mannequins lurch from doorways and windows, lecherous monsters with no legs or only legs, no heads or blacked-out faces. There are fliers stuck on crumbling walls that bear the reminder: *Do Not Spit.*

At the end of the road is Star Music, where Sinjin, Abdullah, and Liam are standing out front. We graduated from high school together a couple of years ago and the three of them today look much as they did when we were students. Sinjin sits slumped against the wall of the store, hands shoved into his pockets. Liam is hopping up and down, curb to street, blowing smoke rings above his head and telling everyone to look. And Abdullah sits on the curb, looking at Liam the way that he always looks at Liam.

When Liam sees me, he stops, his lean, freckled face falling into an expression of shock. 'Astaghfirullah, dead woman walking.'

'Is it true?' Abdullah asks, getting to his feet.

'We heard it was a truck that ran you down,' Sinjin says. 'Was it a truck?'

'If it was a truck, she'd be dead.'

'People are saying she *is* dead.' Liam peers at my face, wincing at what he finds.

'Do you remember anything about it?'

'Should you be out? Don't you need to stay in hospital?'

'I'm fine,' I say. But then I think of the heart beating in my mouth. My mother used to wash my mouth out with soap when she thought I was lying – the memory of it comes back to me now: the rank floral note of lavender, the oily slick the soap would make of my drool. I reach up to find the sorest point on my jaw and I begin to knead at it with my knuckles, focusing my mind on the pain, telling myself that I will not vomit at their feet.

'Remember the little monkey?'

'She was run over, too. Last year, wasn't it?'

'Yeah, wearing a dress.'

'No, a yellow smock and a tiny diaper.'

'And its poor head all busted open on the curb.'

'Like a watermelon exploded.'

'Blood everywhere.'

A fist bangs against the shop window and we all jump.

From inside, the shopkeeper shouts at us to stop loitering and move along.

I trail behind as we make our way to the end of the street, wondering why I am following them, why I have come out tonight at all. Abdullah, gentle and sad and desperate to be liked, is listening patiently as Liam describes the exact color and consistency of the dead monkey's brains. Liam, as he parses the exact shade of pinky-grey – sickly, he muses, but not exactly – is loud, as he almost always is. His hair sticks out like jittery fingers from his skull. Sinjin is trying to get a word in, his plaintive voice launching itself into the scrum every time there is a lull, but no one listens to him.

When we reach his corner – and they are all his corners – we pass Green Jack standing in the puddle of luminosity cast by the sign of a fried chicken franchise. The goldenrod glow of neon on his tattered green clothes transforms him into the street's singular event. For a moment, as he tells the world his visions of strangest truth, he is all anyone on the street knows. As I pass, he holds his hand up to his heart and bows.

Abdullah had asked me if I remembered anything about the accident. I do. There are images so clear they are stitched into my eyes: the black length of the quickly rising street, the sudden upheaval of sky, and a wild, sickening tumble of color as I slammed into the ground.

And before that, too. From just before I stepped off the curb, there is something else that I remember: the sudden appearance of a sharp crack in the guts of the world and a filament of yellow light pouring into the darkness.

And then, just days later, there was Al Ghareeb coming down the street, his eyes full of recognition. Memories are coming back to me now, memories of the stories I told when I was a child about the being I sometimes called Al Ghareeb and sometimes called The Stranger, stories I told in Arabic and English, mixing the languages until I couldn't tell the difference between the two anymore.

When The Stranger roamed the streets looking for a home, he did it with a cool, careless arrogance, and he did his roaming on legs that ended in the sharp, clattering hooves of a goat. He came from the sea, he smelled of salt, and I didn't know if he could even speak.

Liam is still going on about the dead monkey, describing how it looked like a miniature furred person with its limbs and its small dead face, but Sinjin starts talking over him, getting louder with every sentence, determined not to be ignored any longer. He is worried about his job at a property office, certain he is about to lose it. His voice is wretched, as if there is something we could do about the situation if only he could make us pity him enough. If he does lose his job, he says, he is convinced he won't be able to find another, which means he will lose his visa. And if he loses his visa, he will have to go back home.

'I haven't been back to Kerala in years. *Years*,' he says, turning to each of us in turn. 'All I remember is a few visits when I was a kid. I remember getting sick and spending the entire month on the toilet. And this park, I remember this park near my auntie's house, that had pedal boats shaped like swans – but the swans had teeth. *Teeth*.'

Sinjin goes on about these swans and their teeth, about the dreams he had of them biting through the roof of his auntie's house, and the way he would wake up shouting for his mother, but none of us are listening. We've heard it, or stories like it, too many times before, whenever people we knew had to leave for good. As their fathers lost their jobs, as they grew too old to remain on their parents' visas, as they went away to school and never returned.

Finally, Liam interrupts Sinjin's frantic monologue: 'Give it a rest. It's the same for all of us.'

Sinjin looks at Abdullah. 'Not *all* of us.'

'Abdullah might not have to leave like we will,' Liam concedes, 'but he's got problems of his own. The other day we were getting coffee and Abu Talal heard Abdullah say something in Arabic and Abu Talal threatened to run us out of his shop.'

'He told me to not even think about coming back,' Abdullah says, 'until I found a proper tongue.'

Liam makes a playful grab at Abdullah's face, asking if he has found himself one yet. We work our way through a clot of people waiting in line for tikka, and Sinjin tries to pick up the thread of his Keralan memories, describing in detail the sound of wet leaves dripping condensation onto damp soil and the taste of his grandmother's prawn curry, but he says he can never tell if the details of what he remembers are actually true or just snatches of cobbled-together half-memories that he has built up until they feel like fact.

'When I think about it too much, it starts to seem like Kerala isn't even a real place,' he says. 'Like, it's just a place my parents talk about, only they've talked about it so much that I started to believe in it.'

'The last time I went back to Belfast,' Liam says, 'I stood there, in the absolute pissing down rain, thinking fuck me, is this *really* where I'm from?'

'It could be worse, right?' Abdullah asks, dodging around a rough patch in the pavement.

'Yes,' I say. 'It could all be much worse.'

'What I mean is, it's about making a choice,' Abdullah continues, as if he hasn't heard me. 'About where you want to be and how you want to be when you're there. Making that choice and then living with the consequences.'

'What choice?' Sinjin asks. 'I was born here. There was no choice about it.'

Liam claps a hand on the back of Sinjin's neck. 'If you start up again about the swans and their goddamn teeth, I swear I will shove you into traffic.' Then he turns to me, a look of mock chagrin on his face. 'Too soon?'

'All I'm saying,' Sinjin says, holding up his hands in a gesture of surrender, 'is that when the time comes, it's hard to think of leaving. No matter how much I try, it's like I can't imagine what's going to happen next.'

To this, none of us have anything to say. We wait in silence on the corner for a break in the traffic, and, when it comes, we all cross together. Just as we reach the other side, we hear from behind us the lonely sound of Green Jack shouting at the moon.

Bishts and abayas lift in the wind as people stream into the wedding tent at the end of the street. There are faint strains of Egyptian love ballads and the rich smell of roasting lamb in the air. A tent flap opens and out comes a lanky teenage boy with two front teeth made of gold. Seeing Abdullah, he smiles and waves. Abdullah tells us the boy is his cousin, and we follow him toward the tent, where the boy with the two gold teeth insists that we come inside. It doesn't matter that we weren't invited, he says, we are welcome. As I move past him into the clamor of the tent, the boy with the gold teeth sees my face and he recoils.

Inside, there are women crowding the buffet, children dancing in front of the stage, old men smoking in the corner, boys pelting black olives into their mouths, a squall of babies up too late, and a DJ swiveling his snaky hips. Faded rugs cover the harsh pavement of the street and round tables are scattered throughout the makeshift space. I watch a trio of little girls eating handfuls of baklava from the buffet table before their nannies appear, in blue and pink uniforms, to hustle them back to their tables, telling them in Tagalog to sit still and be good. Along the tent's edge tall mabkhara emit twisting swathes of bukhoor smoke, filling the tent with the heady scent of oud. Guests stop and waft clouds of it into their garments, lifting the hems of shawls and gutras to bring the scent close to the skin.

On stage, the bride and groom sit on thrones surrounded by a vivid jungle of flowers and ferns. The groom is sharply handsome, nodding to the crowd, lifting up his glass of carrot juice to toast anyone who walks by. His ivory-colored bisht is edged in thick gold embroidery that hangs heavily down the front of his chest. The bride's hands are painted with henna in designs that swirl up her arms in a succession of stars and flowers, sky and earth.

Liam and Abdullah slip into the crowd while Sinjin and I find seats at a table in the corner. An ornate explosion of white roses gushes from a vase at the center of the table, and beneath the canopy of leaves and petals there is a small hillock of individually wrapped boxes of chocolates.

We both take several. Sinjin eats his methodically and then begins to gnaw on his bottom lip, working the cushion of it back and forth between his teeth. He glances up at me a few times and then fiddles with one of the empty chocolate boxes, opening and closing it, his long fingers making a mess of the delicate design.

'Are you sure you're alright?' he asks.

I chew my piece of chocolate, find that it is filled with a cloying rose jam, and say nothing. I don't like the way Sinjin is looking at me, big eyes blinking behind his glasses.

'Everyone has a different theory about what happened,' he continues.

I keep my eyes on the remaining box in my hands. I pinch one side of it and gently prise open the other. Inside is a morsel of white chocolate shaped like a heart. Not a real heart with the tortured tributaries of veins and chambers, but the symbolic kind, the one that is perfect with symmetry.

'Some say it was a construction truck. Other people say it was a taxi or one of those school shuttles. And other people, well, other people say…' Sinjin stops and shifts in his chair.

There is a sound like thunder, an eruption of voices. The DJ cuts the music and people turn, expectant. A tent flap flies open and into the tent streams a group of men wearing brown and silver daghla over white thobes. Some of them carry drums – daf, darbuka, and tabla – that they pummel and shake in hectic rhythms. The wedding guests whoop and holler, children swarm, women ululate; even the bride is now on her feet. The leader of the troupe guides his men on a circuitous path through the crowd, singing in a piercing voice that his men echo back in haunting unison. It is an old pearl-diving song, sung on dhows long ago, and the lyrics are about the dangers of the sea, the bravery of the divers, and about the hopes they all have of one day returning to land.

In the thick of the crowd, I see Liam and Abdullah, clapping their hands and bending their knees to mimic the performers. One of the troupe members, leathery daf drum in hand, rattles it for them, urging them on in the flickering light. I catch sight of their limbs in flashes, their faces in flashes, the flare of their cigarettes in flashes.

I turn back to Sinjin. 'Do you remember Al Ghareeb?'

Sinjin rips his chocolate foil wrapper in two and nods. 'You told us that story about him that made Hebah cry. We were in the Pyramid, I think.'

'But,' I continue, 'have you ever seen anyone who looks like him?'

'In real life?'

And what *is* real life? I want to ask. But I just nod.

Sinjin frowns and watches me carefully.

In the flickering light of the wedding tent his glasses have become like mirrors. In them, my face looks small and very far away. A waiter rushes past our table carrying a tray of waraq enab. The smell of vinegar catches in the air and makes my eyes water, through the haze of tears the lights in the tent break apart.

'Everything feels strange,' I say.

'It's the end of the world,' Sinjin says. 'Everything *is* strange.'

57 Days

When I wake, a huge sunset fills my room, as if a planet has come to share my space. I am porous, permeable, a cathedral of open doors. I lift my hand toward the red light painting the walls and I wait to feel something. My fingers dip in and out of the ruddy glow, changing color, fading from root to tip, but there is nothing to touch, no sensation to trouble my body. Perhaps I have discovered a fissure in reality, and all I have to do now is let myself tumble through. I wonder if on the other side I would hear the clatter of small black hooves and find that Al Ghareeb is waiting there for me.

In minutes, the planet vanishes and the room descends into a dense blue darkness. I kick away the sheet that has wound itself around my ankles and go to the kitchen. I am thirsty; I have had no water for a thousand years. At the tap I drink my fill, cupping water in my palms and holding it up to my mouth. The water here is hard, filled with minerals and salt. They say it rots your guts and deforms your bones. It is warm and tastes of the sea.

Outside on the street, I find that things are different: the temperature has finally broken, winter is on its way. The crowd pushing down the sidewalk is senseless with joy, welcoming the relief of the cold. At the end of the street, I see Liam and Abdullah bundled in coats, slipping into a Gujarati restaurant, followed by Sinjin who looks flushed in a bulky polo neck. They look right at me before going inside. I see their eyes in quick succession, but they don't smile or wave. They turn and vanish behind the door, which is wrapped in garlands of fake jasmine and red strands of lights. Someone in the crowd behind me laughs, a raucous guffaw that turns into a cough, and I tuck my chin into my chest and keep walking.

Omar told me to take all the time off work that I needed, and Dr Ashguf said I should rest for at least ten days, but my body walks me to the office out of habit. I move through streets that cross like arms over empty lots, and I pass shop windows where necklaces gleam like wet teeth. Doors open and close like mouths and sidewalks are throat-slick with rivulets of spit. Tonight, the whole world is a body.

Escape Now is closed, as it always is at this hour, and I stop on the sidewalk out front to look at the new posters Omar has had put in the window. He likes to say these posters draw customers into the trap, and insists that during the winter people only want to see tropical beaches and sun-drenched cabanas – the posters now advertise Key West, the Seychelles, and the Maldives. I stare at rapturous families dipping their feet into the turquoise splendor of tropical oceans and leaving trails of footprints on white beaches. Behind the colorful posters, the two windows of Escape Now are cavernous and dark. I find my key and enter.

There is not much to do; I don't even think my absence has been felt. I begin with a quick pass through the cubicles, collecting stray invoices, receipts, and booking forms to file. Dana's desk is overrun with plants, climbing vines, and tiny exotic orchids in delicate vases. I water them, pluck at dead leaves, and push them to where I think they will get the best chance at morning sun. Once, when Dana went on holiday, I took all of her plants home with me. There, I watered them carefully and spoke to them, arranging them around my bed like an audience. When she returned and asked where they were, I lied and told her they had all died. Leaf rot, I said, describing a creeping malady that left desiccated leaves in its wake. Days later, I found brown spots across my stolen plants and, within a week, they were all dead.

In the corner by Ali's desk, I spray air freshener, as I always do, although nothing ever takes hold enough to drive away the stench of greasy meat and onions from a long-ago platter of spilled kabsa. Omar even had the carpet replaced, but nothing seems to work. Ali insists it was a djinn's doing – he says he attracts their mischief through no fault of his own. When he was young, he toddled into his family's kitchen when the maid wasn't paying attention and pulled a pot of boiling water off the stove, scalding his face and leaving burns on his back. It was clearly the work of a djinn. Ever since, Ali says he has been stalked by misfortune.

Next, I refill the paper in the fax machine, tidy the supply cupboard, and take stock of what in the kitchen needs replacing. There is a sour smell coming from the refrigerator and, jammed in the very back, I find a carton of expired laban and throw it out. In Omar's office, I water the nodding ferns along his windowsill and refill the sweet lemon candies that he keeps in a ceramic jar on the edge of his desk. When he interviewed me for this job, two years ago, he insisted I leave with a handful, telling me to always take more whenever I wanted.

I had just returned to the souq after my brief months away in America and rumors were running thick in the street. Children whispered 'majnoona' when I passed the playgrounds, and, when they were feeling bold, they experimented with English and called me crazy. Omar had graciously pretended to be unaware of all of that. He sat me down in his office, settling himself on his leather sofa, and said that he couldn't pay much, but the job wasn't taxing and would only require a few hours a day. He even hinted that while I was still currently young enough to be on my father's visa, when the time came in a few years for me to need a visa of my own he would do what he could to sponsor me so I could stay. The time for that becoming a necessity is now fast approaching, but I don't know if it will even be possible. And, if it isn't, I also don't know if it will be possible for me to leave.

During that interview, when I asked Omar if I could come in and do all the work at night, when no one else was here, there had been a moment when his round, cheery face looked concerned and I thought he was going to say no. But his smile quickly returned and he said that I could do whatever was best for me. When he pushed his hand into the jar of plastic-wrapped candies to get my handful, instead of feeling grateful to be offered a job that I didn't deserve, I found myself hating him for his pity.

The last thing I do before I leave is carry a large cardboard box of new destination brochures into the filing room. Filing paperwork, and organizing these brochures, is the bulk of my job, and I save it for last because I like the way the filing room feels like a hollow somewhere deep within the center of the earth. I take a breath, wanting to speak, wanting to hear the flatness of my voice in this small space, but nothing comes out. My tongue is a dry piece of clay in a riverbed. I long for water. I bend down and tear a hole into the top of the cardboard box; the black gape of it reminds me of a mouth, open and shrieking.

56 Days

The new god has drawn people from all over the world to the souq. Sitting on the curb in front of my apartment building, I grind a knuckle into the most painful part of my jaw, working it into a solid wail of agony, while I watch the tour guide lead another group of tourists toward the archeological site at the end of the street. The tourists walk slowly, their faces set in frowns. This isn't the archeological site they are interested in; it has nothing to do with the new god.

One of the tourists, an older woman in frayed shorts, legs lined with blue veins, asks the guide if he is certain the water chamber site isn't open yet. When he says he is certain, she asks if an exception could be made just this once. After all, they have come this far. When he apologizes and says no, the woman begins muttering about this new god and how suspicious it all is. 'We've come all this way and yet we can't see it,' she says, 'doesn't that seem wrong to you?'

It appears that no one is quite sure what to make of the new god. The only person who seems to really believe is the archeologist who discovered the tablet at the water chamber site that he thinks changes everything. The newspaper article that announced his new theory wasn't run on the front page but was buried in the culture section, and the headline didn't trumpet so much as muse: *New Ancient God?*

The photograph of the archeologist, Elias Haddad, that accompanied the article showed a man in his fifties standing stiffly on the uppermost stone step of the water chamber in the palm grove. His stern face served as a rebuke to the tentative headline, grey fronds of unkempt hair sprouted from his chin and brows, and his clear blue eyes were fierce. It had been several years since I had seen him – that first and only time – but in the photograph I saw that he was unchanged. His hair slightly longer, his waist slightly thinner, but, essentially, he was the same.

It was unequivocal, he was quoted as saying. The ancient god of the waters and chaos, long believed by scholars to be a single deity, was actually two: the god of the waters *and* the god of chaos. Now that he was known, the god of chaos could stand alone.

Stopping at the small archeological site at the end of my street, the tour guide pauses, waiting for the group to cohere. He looks familiar. Tall and broad with black curls, he reminds me of a bear with his sad face and sloping shoulders. When the group surrounds him and falls silent, he lifts a foot and lets it hang there for a moment before lowering it gently, elegantly, to the ground.

'Right here, on this very spot, for more than four thousand years, people have lived and died. People have been born, people have fallen in love, people have dreamed and mourned, raised their families, made their lives.'

I stop working at my aching jaw and get up and join the group, placing myself between a gaunt bald man and a square woman wearing a pink beret. An elderly couple at the front of the group crane their necks to look around the guide and see the lot behind him. Small, ringed with a rustic wooden fence, and adrift with scrubby bushes and tattered newspapers, the space does not look like one worthy of attention. To one side is Clean Boy Laundry and to the other Abdul Abdul Tailors.

The tour guide continues, his voice a thick strand of cotton wool amid the din of the street. He tells us that the small depressions in the center of the lot, square-shaped and demarcated with small stones, indicate where ancient homes used to stand. He describes the way the homes were laid out, where people placed their beds, their cooking pits, their food storage. The ancients lived lives that were not unlike ours, he says, eyeing each person in the group.

When I played in this dirt lot as a child, no tour groups ever came. Damp patches in the corner smelled of old urine, and stray cats gave birth to sickly kittens in the brush. I would stroll through the footprints of the homes and rearrange the small stones as I saw fit, deciding two rooms should be one, or kitchens should be bedrooms, outlining a life for myself that was entirely my own.

'So, do you believe this so-called new god is a legitimate discovery or not?' one of the tourists asks the guide, interrupting his speech. She has a cap of blonde curls and lips painted a deep purple to match the cotton tunic she wears.

'I heard that some people are saying it's a hoax,' remarks the gaunt man next to me.

The woman in shorts speaks up: 'It could be an etymological difference, couldn't it? It isn't as clear as saying definitively there is a new god simply based on a single tablet, right? It's just simply *not* how it is done.'

The tour guide frowns at the interruption and says that the experts must interpret whatever they find as best they can. 'When something is as far gone from us as the ancient past, maybe all we can do is live with the uncertainty.'

The woman with the purple lips scowls. No one wants to be on this street, at this site, where nothing important ever happened. Just lives upon lives.

Shopkeepers have begun to emerge from their shops and they are prowling at the edge of the group, wondering if they can make a quick sale before the tourists move on. One of them, Liacut, a man I've known my whole life, holds a white pashmina in front of my face, saying he will give me a special price.

The guide's voice carries on: 'It is fascinating, is it not, to think of a god being forgotten for so long? If, over the course of a few thousand years, something so important can vanish from human knowledge, think what else might slip our collective mind. Think, for example, of the people who lived in these homes here. We don't even know their names.'

His voice drops and he asks us to close our eyes and imagine something. All around me the tourists cross their arms, sigh, and then they let their eyelids drop. In contrast to their sunburned faces, the sudden bleak whiteness of their eyelids is troubling. Watching them like this, so vulnerable and so unaware, makes my heart feel loose in my chest. I wonder what I could do to them.

'Let us imagine our own past,' the guide says. 'I could think of my family. My mother and father, my siblings. I could remember special days, like Eids and birthdays. Or maybe I could think about friendships, quarrels, illnesses. All of these things feel real to me, very urgent, like they could never be forgotten. And yet, I know that in time they will be.'

The tour guide is looking at me now, his gaze settling on my bruised face like a bird coming to land on a branch.

I stare back. He is wrong about time, I want to tell him, and he is wrong about the past. I think about saying it, shouting it maybe, so that the tourists would jump, dropping their tacky souvenirs on the ground. Open your eyes, I would say, nothing is ever really over.

Eventually, the tourists shift on their feet, their eyes blink open, and they mumble to one another. They are bored, and this is weird. They see the shops, the shopkeepers, the wares, and they begin to drift. Overhead, the moon sails free from a gauze of cloud and the sky swells with light.

The woman in purple gathers her two young sons, both slowly making their way through falafel sandwiches, and she asks if I will take their picture. Between bites of his sandwich, the littlest boy reaches up to rub at a red mark on his cheek.

Through the viewfinder, the figures of the mother and her two sons look outlandishly large against the small, dusty site. Their smiles are broad and bored. I think about asking them how they can smile when death exists.

I snap the photo and the mother snatches the camera from my hands without saying thank you. She hurries her boys past me, her purple lips pinched, and I fear I may have spoken my question out loud.

=

When I was seven years old my father called me into his study. I did not enter that room often. He taught at the international high school and this was the room where he planned his classes, graded papers, and read his books. Entering the room's darkened hush, and standing amid the

Persian rugs haphazardly nailed to the wall and the drifts of loose papers molting like feathers from every surface, I felt exposed. As if I had stepped into a clearing and in the surrounding shadows everything was made of eyes.

'What do you think?' asked my father, nodding to a small clock lying on the floor in the center of the room.

I thought the clock looked like the sick and dying cats I would see sometimes on the street, vulnerable out in the open where they should not be. I didn't know what to say, so I stayed silent.

Sitting behind his large desk my father looked small. He was a small man made of circles: the round bald dome of his skull, his round blue eyes, and the round paunch of his waist. I thought of him as a collection of marbles. Into the silence came a noise from the other end of our flat – the quiet thrum of music on the radio from the room where my mother did her painting.

My father's eyes shifted upward to settle on something perched atop the bookshelf. I followed his gaze and found another clock, identical to the one on the floor.

For a moment, I thought he had done a magic trick, some kind of sleight of hand whereby he had transported the original clock from the floor to the shelf.

'Two clocks in two different places,' he said. 'Tell me, do you think they are keeping the same time?'

I thought carefully and answered yes.

Steepling his small fingers, my father nodded. 'And why do you think that?'

'Because time is time. It doesn't matter where you put a clock, time is the same everywhere.'

He smiled and I took a step backward, closer to the door.

Breaking apart the steeple of his hands, he lifted a finger into the air. 'It might not seem logical, but the fact of the matter is the clock on top of the bookshelf is running ever so slightly faster than the clock on the floor. Of course, these clocks are too rudimentary to capture this, but with advanced enough timepieces, say atomic clocks, and especially over much greater distances, like a clock at the top of a tall mountain, the difference is demonstrable.'

I looked at the clock on the bookshelf and then at the clock on the floor. I wanted to tell my father that I didn't believe him, that this could not be true, but I knew saying that would end everything.

My father leaned forward over his desk and as he looked at me, I had the feeling that even though I was standing directly in front of him, he couldn't see me. I thought I could take a step to my left or to my right and his eyes would not move, they would remain staring into the space where I had just been.

'So, the question arises: which of these times is correct? Is the clock on the floor accurate, or the one up on the shelf?'

I looked down at the clock on the rug and felt sorry for how it was so conspicuously out of place. 'The one on the floor?'

'Let us return to your answer to the original question,' he said. 'You said time is the same everywhere. This is wrong. You are wrong. Time is not the same everywhere. These two clocks are each in their own times. In fact, you and I are in our own times. There is no right or wrong – time is different at every point in the universe.'

He began explaining something called relativity, telling

me that time was not absolute, that it changed depending on factors like speed, acceleration, and gravity. And it wasn't just our perception of time that changed, he emphasized, but actual time itself.

He mentioned the Al Bushra family, who lived in the apartment directly below us. They were actually slightly younger than us, he explained, just by virtue of spending much of their lives closer to the ground. Up here, on the third floor, our time was ticking away that little bit faster.

'In fact,' my father continued, 'if we dig deeper, we find that time is far stranger than we imagine. Just as there is no constant tick of a universal clock, time does not even move inexorably forward.'

I didn't understand this word, 'inexorable'. It sounded painful and it made me think of all the times my mother took me to the hospital. I imagined sharp objects slicing into soft flesh.

But my father did not pause to ask if I needed anything explained. He continued, saying that some people – he gestured vaguely to the books and papers that surrounded him – think that we live in a universe in which all time, past, present, and future, happens simultaneously. We only conceive of time moving in a straight line because of our own feeble perceptions.

'We see time as shooting relentlessly forward, like a flying arrow, because of our own clouded view of processes we can only dream of grasping. Think about it,' he said: 'have you ever been in the past? Truly? Or in the future? Or, is it more accurate to say, that you have only ever been in the present? That we all live in our own individual perpetual nows?'

There was a weight to this that felt like truth. I wondered

if this was a conversation every child had at some point with their father.

From the other side of the flat, the music shifted momentarily, sliding between stations – the sound of garbled voices, a shout, the cry of a stringed instrument – before picking up again. I wondered what time the radio was living in, where it was in relation to me, and where we would end up if there was no future. Then there was the sharp thud of a slamming door and the music was gone.

55 Days

I dream of the new ancient god birthing himself from the other: what was one, is now two. The world, it seems, is full of new divinity. This one has lain in wait for four thousand years and now he will stalk the streets. When he opens his mouth, a lusty cry will color the air and flowers will bloom in the sky.

While I slept the earth reoriented itself in space and when I wake I find a world gone heavy with meaning. I shiver in tangled sheets and, when I swallow, I taste something that might be blood. There is a man made of rocks living on the streets and I do not want to know him now. Night is certain and it is all around, fierce in its dark totality. I have not seen proper daylight in weeks and I am not convinced it even still exists. How to believe that daytime people swarm above ground beneath a monstrous star? I feel myself fall away.

54 Days

I do not leave my bed. A headache grinds behind my eyes and waves of dizziness come and go like erratic tides. I wonder if it is the wounds that litter my body, if they have gone bad and sickness is percolating through the currents of my blood. But before I can grab hold of that thought, I feel myself being carried away over vast distances, across geographies that never fully resolve. Beneath me, landscapes shudder like lightning, green seas capsize continents, and the depths beneath the world are revealed: there is something emerging. I sense claws and teeth and a great hunger. The word 'disturbances' rises in my mind. I sleep and wake and thirst.

From my bed I can see a pile of mail in the entry way, a small batch of envelopes that must have been dropped through the letterbox by the postman sometime during the day while I was sleeping. There are menus, bills, and at the very top, like a bird sitting on a clutch of eggs, is perched a putty-pink envelope. Getting up, moving slowly, placing my feet deliberately to fight off the peaks and valleys of vertigo, I make my way to the front door and lean over the pile. When the handsome canting leftward-leaning script on the putty-pink envelope resolves itself in my eyes, my body reacts instantly. My left leg kicks out and the pink envelope spins across the tiles and vanishes into the darkness beneath my bed.

For a moment, I stand there, watching where it has gone, the room lurching around me. Heart stuttering against ribs – too fast, too fast, too fast – I wait for the letter to emerge. I imagine it pulling itself back into the light to confront me, propelled by the need of the person who has sent it. I even hear a familiar voice emerging from inside, imploring, begging, sobbing, and smell the scent of linseed oil and turpentine, cigarette smoke and hibiscus tea.

I am running down the apartment block stairs before I can stop myself, my feet hammering the unfinished cement. On the second floor there is the smell of cooking – onions, ghee, cardamom – and on the first floor there is the sound of a child singing, their voice thick with phlegm. Only on every other landing is there a full complement of light bulbs, so I pass through a succession of light and darkness as I descend, snapping in and out of existence.

Bursting onto the street, there is panic in me like a heated pebble, ricocheting through my body, lancing off organs and skittering across bone. I walk fast to the end of the street, turn the corner fast, and cross the street fast. I walk fast through an alley and faster through an empty lot. Every time I come to the end of a road that leads out of the souq, I smell the sea and turn away.

Tour groups clog the corners, cameras lifted to eyes, waist pouches bulging like exposed intestines. I pass a line of child-sized mannequins propped against their storefront window. Boys, all of them, dressed in formal bishts with silver braids and immaculately arranged gutras. The pious shopkeeper has sliced off each boy's face and their white Styrofoam interiors are ragged and stained.

A metallic trill silvers the air. From the darkness at the end of the alley there appears a light. The light hangs, the light hangs, the light hangs. It comes closer. The bicycle attached to the light is old, older than me, older even than the not-very-young man riding it. Black skin, white hair, and red betel nut-stained teeth. He rings his bell again and, as he passes me, he swerves. For a moment, a gravitational well opens between us two planets spinning in this uncanny night. As we pass the zenith of our mutual orbit, he looks up at me and I see that he knows the street, he knows time itself. Again, the sound of his bell, bright and cold, and then the gravity between us breaks and he is gone.

In the silence, I know everything has changed. I become very aware of the darkness of this empty street and the way it presses up against me like a living thing.

Then I hear a sound.

At first, it is the distant drop of a falling rock, something small and faint. But then the sound repeats, growing louder and closer with each repetition. I recognize these pebble-dropping sounds that are no longer the sounds of pebbles dropping. The cadence is familiar: it is, I realize, the making of a creature pulling itself through these narrow lanes. It is the stately pacing of sharp hooves.

And then, in the gloom at the end of the street, I see a figure. In the sliver of darkness between two streetlights, he stands, immobile, watching. I think I see the rolling sweep of searchlight eyes.

For the second time tonight, I run.

Turning down a succession of corners, I am soon lost in a web of residential streets. On either side of me the buildings are tall and looming, and rushing through them is like being pulled under water, into sudden silence, into submarine darkness. There are no streetlights, no car horns, no wailing children. At a corner with no street signs, I stop and bend at the waist, hands on my knees, trying to control the heaving in my mind. I can smell the sea, the churning salt desolation of it. I have gone too far.

When I hear the hooves closing in, I try to run again, but the pain is too great, my heels hitting the pavement send flashes from my jaw into my head, into my eyes, filling the world with buzzing lights. I choke back a scream. I tell myself there is no reason to flee – he is not real; he cannot lace his fishbone fingers through my heart.

One more turn and I am faced with a dead-end alley. At the head is a coral stone wall splattered with graffiti. In the center, someone has left a scrawl of purple spray paint, a single giant eye. There is nowhere left for me to go. I turn around and remember all the things I ever said about Al Ghareeb, the way he tumbled upward from the bottom of the sea to find the shore, the way his loneliness is like a living thing propelling him forward, never allowing him to rest. The click of hooves is uneven, his stride is lopsided, sickly, and I wonder what has happened to him out here on the streets.

The figure that turns the corner is shrouded in black and her face is knit with shadow. She walks slowly, pain twisting somewhere deep inside, holding her left leg a few inches short of a full stride. On her feet are sandals with pink plastic heels: click clack, click clack. She makes her way to a door in the middle of the alley. It is acid green, like the rags Green Jack wears, like something radioactive leaking out of another dimension. She finds her key, unlocks the door, and then turns to look at me over her shoulder.

'Masa al khair,' I say, stilling the tremble in my throat.

'You shouldn't lurk,' she says. 'What kind of trouble do you want?'

I do not know how to tell her that I am running from a man with the legs of a goat who I made up half a lifetime ago, a man who lives in the ocean and emerges dripping at night to roam the streets and look for a home to call his own.

She clucks her tongue. 'There is a man made of rocks out on the streets tonight. If you don't want any trouble, you should keep yourself at home.'

'What – what did you say?'

She leans forward and tips her face to the ground. Something has gone wrong – she is falling and I have to catch her. But then I see that she is only looking down at my feet. When I follow her gaze, I realize I am not wearing any shoes. I have left my flat in my bare feet and the skin of them is now hatch-marked with scratches and scrapes. Turning to look behind me, I see that in my wake I have left a trail of footsteps rimmed with blood.

53 Days

There is an antiques store that features in its window an oil painting of a woman with doomsday breasts. I stand in front of her now, eyeing the nipples that goad like eyes. The figure is reclining on a chartreuse chaise longue that I have never seen before, and I do not know if the artist imagined it or simply borrowed it for the painting. Her long eyes gaze toward the ceiling, martyrlike, besieged by all that she knows. It isn't one of the artist's best works: the strokes are heavy, even clumsy in places, and the colors are tedious mottled browns and predictable blues. It is only the breasts that mean anything.

I stand here staring for a stretch of time that I do not entirely understand. I am still permeated with memories, so I tell myself that bodies are just ways for time to understand itself and the memories can come and go as they please. In the corner of the painting, I see that the artist's signature has changed – what used to be neat and small is here a disorganized sprawl that jags off the canvas.

The street that houses the antiques shop is quiet. A few taxis roll by, a motorcycle, a nurse carrying an empty bird cage. A cool wind brings a soft green wave of fecundity, and I take one last look at the painting and leave the shop behind. I follow the scent of frangipani and lemon trees, date palms and night-blooming jasmine, feeling the microscopic spores from the inner sanctum of the plants laying their claim inside my lungs. They funnel into the deltas of my alveoli, spreading their fingers into all the spaces of my body. In a hundred years there will be an oasis in my blood.

Al Hadiqa emerges from the darkness like a whale breaching from the deep – a vast muscular behemoth of vegetal green and fertile darkness surrounded by squat apartment buildings. No one remembers who started the garden. It could have been Sangeetha the nurse from Dhaka, Brad the bartender from Ottawa, or Hussain the taxi driver from Baghdad. No one knows, and whoever it was left years ago. The garden began as nothing more than a dirt lot, empty save for a lone banyan tree. Then, Sangeetha or Brad or Hussain planted a circle of bougainvillea. Just bougainvillea, nothing more. Eventually, the flowers took hold and grew into a spiral of thick, sturdy bushes: pink and white and yellow.

When they finally moved on, Sangeetha or Brad or Hussain, instead of leaving Al Hadiqa to die, a dozen families took on the garden. The original banyan tree and bougainvillea bushes were joined by jasmine vines, silver sage, oleander, aloe, palm trees, pink tea roses, winding raked dirt paths, and low wooden benches. Now, children gather in the morning before school to throw banyan berries at each other, men sneak forbidden cigarettes in the dense cover during long Ramadan days, and Malak, whenever her mother can be left alone for a few hours, comes to stand at the garden's very center and recite poetry.

I find Malak here now, standing on her stool beneath a lofty palm, a clutch of papers in hand, her angry voice blazing out into the night. She is reading a poem about heaven's vault of lapis lazuli, about a distracted, lovelorn heart, about questions begged from lost souls wandering by the sea.

The gathered crowd appears to me first as muddled faces swimming up from the deep darkness. When I can see them all, I see that there are many, maybe two dozen, lounging beneath the berry-dropping banyan trees and the swaying clematis vines. I sit among them and watch as Malak leans forward, straining her neck, thrusting her chest to expand her voice. She is ugly and electric, and the silver threads knotted into her headscarf spark in the light as if she is about to go up in flames.

When the poem finishes, she totters for a moment on the edge of her stool. Then her face drains of intensity and even the sparking silver threads reflect no more light. People clear their throats and begin to talk, hoping she is finished. She is. She gets down, picks up her stool, and turns to go home. I go with her.

We walk through the density of Al Hadiqa with all its dank botanic smells – the mineral stench of soil, the beckoning allure of jasmine, the reek of wild garlic. Once at Malak's apartment building, we ascend four flights of stairs, past doorways painted blue and black, past railings hung with garlands of plastic flowers.

Inside her flat, we find her mother wheezing on the sofa. She tries to stand up to greet me, but Malak tells her no and I bend to her instead.

'Ahlan wa sahlan.'

'Ahlan biki.'

'Kef halik habibti?'

'Wallah alhamdulillah. Kefik enti?'

'Wallahi alhumdulillah.'

Our greeting unspools for some time, punctuated by cheek kisses and the holding of hands. Before she became ill, Um Malak ran a school, and she still speaks to everyone like she is speaking to a small child – looking earnestly into my face and clutching my hands, her words are slow and perfectly formed. She drifts sometimes into the language of her childhood, which I don't understand, but, if I keep nodding, she eventually finds her way back to Arabic or English. When I sit next to her on the sofa, she hands me a ginger-chew from a plastic bowl on the cluttered side table. Next to the bowl, I can see a nebulizer, several bottles of pills, a box of tissues covered in a white doily, and a laminated sheet containing a list of phone numbers, including the doctor, pharmacist, and three different ambulance services.

Um Malak tells me that she heard about my accident. She squints at me, assessing the damage. 'You have al-'ayn,' she concludes. 'It's all but certain that someone gave you the evil eye. That's what caused the accident.'

I shake my head. I have nothing to envy. Why would I have al-'ayn?

'You need an egg,' she insists.

I show her my empty hands.

She nods, working her small lips thoughtfully into her teeth, and then she rears her head back and spits on me. The white globule lands on my shoulder and I feel the wet warmth of it through my shirt. Looking down, I see that it is flecked with particles of old food and bits of phlegm.

I thank her.

She nods and tells me I will be alright now, but I must be more careful.

The couch is sealed in plastic that squelches whenever I shift in my seat. The TV remote control is also sealed in plastic, as is the lamp shade, the coffee table, and the two side tables. The apartment is spotlessly clean, with not even a fingerprint smudge on any of the framed pictures lining the walls. Behind each pane of glass is one of Malak's many dead relatives.

The man with the bristling black mustache died in a car accident. The woman perched on a bench at the edge of a snowy hilltop died in some far-flung war. This one died from cancer, this one from heart disease, this one from diabetes, this one in childbirth, and this one from some disease that was like malaria but was not exactly malaria. Dead, dead, dead, all of them dead and forever smiling behind glass, oblivious to their fates, their cancers, their wayward bullets, their sugar in the blood, all gazing out at us in this small apartment that smells of ginger candy and too much Dettol.

In the corner, near the window, I see a photograph I have not noticed before. The window's heavy brocade curtains are tied back with a sash; I see that if they were let down, as usual, the picture would be hidden behind their folds. The frame of this photograph is lighter than the rest, made out of another kind of wood and stained with a gloss that gives it a waxy shine. I cross the room to look closer.

It is black and white and not as clear as the others. It shows a long, dirty street with dingy shop windows and, to one side, a car with no wheels propped up on bricks. There is only a single figure in the street. He stands at the end of the pavement, draped in shadow. His eyes have trapped what little light there is, but the rest of his face is washed in darkness; all of his outlines have bled.

A blade of glass twists in my heart: a man made of rocks is out on the street tonight.

Malak is in the kitchen making tea, so I ask Um Malak who the man in the photograph is.

She turns her head. It takes forever. Centuries pass. When her eyes finally reach mine, I see a thin trickle of drool leaking out of the corner of her mouth.

'Min?'

'This man. Who was he?'

'Min?' she asks again.

'This man here. Standing in the street. I haven't seen this picture before. Who was he?'

Um Malak does not look at the picture, her gaze stays resting on me. It feels heavy, as if a piece of the sky has fallen on my skull. The trickle of drool has reached the edge of her chin. I watch it tremble and wait for it to fall.

'Um Malak, who is he?'

'She doesn't know.' Malak enters from the kitchen carrying a tray of tea and cookies. 'I don't know either. We've just always had the picture. When I was little it gave me nightmares, so Mama hid it behind the curtains. He looks wrong, doesn't he? The eyes, I think.'

Um Malak nods.

'You used to say, Mama, that man can hear me in my dreams. That he could go wherever he wanted. But he's just a man on the street. Dead now, anyway.'

Malak pours the tea into small glasses and insists I take a sweet crumbly mamoul. She holds her mother's tea cup in her hands and blows across the surface of the amber liquid until it has cooled enough to be sipped.

'Did they like your poems, hayati?'

'Yes, Mama.'

'Did they clap for you?'

'Yes, Mama.'

'I thought I heard them clapping.'

'How could you hear them clapping?'

'I left the window open because I knew there would be clapping.'

'You can't leave the window open, Mama.'

'I can and I did.'

'It's not good for you, all that pollution.'

'Ah, pollution is just a made-up word.'

While they talk, I watch the show playing on the television, which is covered along the top in white doilies and a thin sheet of plastic. Two men in white thobes and white taqiyya with gimmicky dentures bulging from their mouths are racing around a small desert town in a beat-up sedan. There has been a mix-up, it seems: the car is not theirs, and the police are after them. The city flashes by through the windows of the car, a blur of white and ochre and beaten black asphalt. Faster and faster they drive, taking turns recklessly, losing their minds with fear. One of the men is yelling, the other sobbing. He sobs so hard he sometimes forgets to drive, lifting his hands into the air, beseeching God for help.

We finish our tea and Malak's mother begins to doze. Her chest lifts and falls rapidly. It has been weeks since I last saw her and she looks worse. She always looks worse. She is thinner, her eyes have sunken yet further into her skull, and I have to stop myself from reaching out to stroke the tender skin of her eyelids. I think of the pink casings of her tired heart and wonder where the meat of her has gone.

Malak takes the cups and plates to the kitchen, and we go into her bedroom. Stepping through the door is like stepping into the center of a giant globe: on every wall, even creeping across the ceiling and lipping up from the floor, there are maps. Maps of the city, maps of the souq, maps of the region, and maps of the distant continents that Malak dreams of someday seeing. Near the door lies the whole of the Pacific, vast swathes of ocean dotted with freckles of land, swooping archipelagos, and spindly isthmuses. North America hulks around the closet, sweeping white tundra and fierce mountain ranges and deserts with valleys named after death. South America winds like a snake next to the bookshelf, dank with steaming jungle and pale blasts of arid plateau. Africa swallows the balcony door – too big for one map, its vast distances are spread across half a dozen. Next to the bed, a map of Australia, so Malak can run her eye around and around the mottled coastline as she drifts to sleep.

Malak spent her childhood making lists of the places she wanted to see, evaluating countries with a complex set of criteria that she never bothered to explain. As soon as we finished school, she used to say, she would be gone. But then her father died. And then her grandparents. And then her maiden aunt and her last elderly cousin. Now, if Malak left, there would be no one to look after her mother. So, Malak stays. She has been staying for years.

From my pocket I pull out a brochure I took from work and hand it to her.

'Easter Island,' she reads, a frown notching a wrinkle between her brows. 'Are these statues real?'

'I think so.'

'I don't have an Easter Island brochure yet.'

'That's why I brought it.'

She gives the brochure a long stare. The statues don't look possible and I know that she is thinking that things like this can't exist. She finally takes it to her closet where she adds it to the stacks that fill the narrow space. They're nearly as tall as she is.

From a desk overflowing with atlases and almanacs, she unearths a crumpled pack of cigarettes that we take onto her small balcony. Now that Mr Milo from next door has moved back to Bangladesh and his apartment is empty, we are free to sit and smoke without him complaining about loose women making spectacles of themselves. Once, I told him the whole world was nothing but spectacle, and he shook his head and looked at me as if he was about to cry.

From the balcony, Al Hadiqa is a thick, frothing ocean of green. Caught in currents of wind, the tops of the trees whip and toss. At the end of the street, Dynamo Computer Goods is flashing with advertisements for their Apocalypse Sale. The windows are plastered with posters: *Y2K NOW! Protect Yourself! Cheat Death!*

'Did you see the paper?' Malak asks. 'About this new god? That's a bad sign, no matter how you look at it. Things like this crawling out of history, that's all the proof you need right there.'

'Proof of what?' I ask.

She juts her chin toward Dynamo Computer Goods. 'Proof of *that*.' Cigarette burning between her teeth, she continues: 'They say that the moment we hit midnight and all the computers short out, airplanes will fall out of the sky, stock markets will collapse, and people will lose everything. Nothing will function. There'll be riots and wars, a total and complete breakdown of society. Imagine if it gets to nuclear weapons. I mean, shit. You just know they're all out there, all over the world, everybody aiming at everybody else, just waiting to hit the button. The clocks will tick over and it will be mayhem.'

She flicks her cigarette over the balcony's edge and we watch its red flame spiral toward the waiting street. Somewhere below us a cat howls and another answers. A snarl, a hiss, a scream.

'How is she doing?' I ask.

'Not long now, apparently. That's what the doctors said, anyway. It could be weeks. The other day she coughed and it was nothing but blood. Have you ever seen blood like that? Coming from a place it shouldn't? It's darker than you'd think.'

Malak folds her legs up and hugs her knees to her chest.

'In the morning,' she continues, 'I sometimes take her tea when she's still in bed, and she'll talk like she doesn't know me. I'm staring right at her and she'll ask me my name. The thing is, though, I don't know if I believe it. There's this look in her eyes. Like she's testing me.'

Down below, a car drives by, leaking music: Fayrouz tripping up and down the scales. Al Hadiqa rustles and grows a shade darker.

Malak stands up. 'I found something that I want to show you.'

She goes inside while I remain on the balcony. The wind is cold, and it solidifies the twisting pain in my leg and in my jaw. I imagine it growing stronger, taking hold and taking root. Staying forever.

When the balcony door slides back open Malak emerges without a face. In its place is the monstrous visage of an insect with bulging black discs for eyes and a mangled rubber mouth. Frayed straps dangle from her chin and lash tightly over the back of her head. From inside, her breath sounds like it is coming from underwater, sludgy and laborious. I think of blood coming from places it shouldn't, gushing too dark from passages not meant to carry it.

=

During the Gulf War, Malak taught me how to predict the future. The war was a season of many times, and at our school everything ground to a halt. So many students had left with their families to seek safety overseas that exams were dispensed with and our curriculum consisted of watching movies and working through spelling notebooks. While out on the street the world moved faster than ever before, at school nothing ever seemed to happen. We dozed at our desks, we reread books from previous years, and we doodled on the chalkboard. The only moments of excitement, when time seemed itself again, were when the air-raid sirens sounded.

When this happened, our teacher would freeze as though she had been caught doing something wrong, and all of us would sit and gape until she sprang back to life shouting for us to get our gas masks on and hide under our desks. Then it was a mad scramble of elbows and knees and canvas straps and cold metal buckles and my mask always catching finnicky and stubborn beneath my chin. It seemed an impossibility that these insect-heads with rubbery plates for eyes and drooping snouts would protect us from the poisons that could fill the air at any time. We wore them like talismans, more than anything, masking ourselves in hope, giggling as we huddled under our desks from the sheer improbable excitement of maybe dying at school with multiplication tables on the chalkboard and cartoon cat posters on the wall.

One day, when we were all hiding beneath our desks as the sirens went on and on until it seemed they were the new sound of the world, like wind itself had been transformed into panic, from her pocket Malak pulled out a complicated square of paper. As I watched, she poked her fingers into its undercarriage and with a quick motion popped the whole thing open. Perching atop her fingers with four sharp peaks, it looked like a strange two-faced creature. It was a fortune teller.

At her urging, I selected a peak with a number written on it. She then flexed and bent her fingers the exact number of times my peak indicated, and ended by splaying them open, revealing the inner world of the fortune teller with colors written on each panel. I chose yellow.

Carefully, she pulled open the panel to reveal my fortune: *You have far to go!*

Beneath our shield of clustered desks, the other students clapped, thrilled by this magic. One by one, Malak went through the rest of the class, pouncing her fingers, unfolding the future: *You will have ten children! You will be a doctor! You will die young!*

It was different when the sirens went off at night when I was home with my parents. Then was the slowest time of all. My mother and father and I would gather in the small bathroom by the front door because that was the only room in the flat without windows, which was supposed to make it safest. My mother was always redecorating, and during the winter of the war the bathroom was done in a South-West Americana theme, with terracotta-colored walls, small cacti in turquoise pots, and hand towels edged with squiggly black sombrero hats. My father had deemed it unbearably tacky.

I wedged myself between the toilet and the bathtub, my mother sat next to the sink, and my father settled by the door. The first thing we did was wet a towel in the tub, wring it out, and jam it in the crack beneath the door and the tile floor. A radio announcement my mother had heard said this would offer an additional layer of protection from possible chemical warfare and so she insisted, even though my father called it hysterical. He spent our time in the bathroom reading, and if my mother or I spoke to him he pretended not to hear. It felt unnatural to sit so close to him. His body was a mystery to me. We never touched, were never near one another for very long, so I would take the chance to study the way he took his breaths and sweated his sweat and crossed his arms.

Sometimes, my mother brought her sketchbook into the bathroom. She would fill pages with rough pencil outlines of paintings she wanted to make, testing angle and perspective, frowning with indecision. She always brought her cigarettes, her monogrammed silver lighter, and her drink. By the end of our time in the bathroom she would have red marks on her chin from lifting the bottom of her mask so she could partake. There was a method to the way she did it that never altered. She was always quick with it, the whole fidgety motion saturated with shame. With her thumb she'd break the seal between the mask and her skin and, with her pointer finger hooked under the rubber, she'd give it a quick yank, exposing thin, questing lips. They reminded me of baby birds huddled in a nest – it was the way they reached out for the cigarette or the rim of her glass, two little birds desperate for something.

I had seen reports on the news of what we were hiding from. Big black sky, rudimentary suggestion of a distant cityscape made of shadow and concrete, and then the bright screams of light as Scud and Patriot missiles battled it out among the stars. Things that on the news went very fast, in real life went very slow. Huddled in the bathroom with my parents, breathing in the clammy air of my gas mask, I could take a thousand breaths, it seemed, before the sirens gave the all clear. I could swallow the spit pooling beneath my tongue a million times, before my mother would decide we could go back to bed. My heart could pound a billion times, while we waited to see if the Scuds would come falling down on us in our windowless bathroom with our wet towel jammed beneath the door. I wondered how it was that time could behave like that, quick and then slow, fast and then faster, then I remembered my father's lessons with the two clocks and I knew that time was revealing itself to me.

On the final occasion that the air-raid sirens sent us to the bathroom, I fell out of time completely. It was so late that it was almost morning, and the sound of the sirens had yanked me from bed still reeling with dreams. Sitting in my place between the toilet and the tub, I watched my mother smoke and my father turn the pages of his book. After some time – minutes or years – their actions developed incompatible rhythms. An exhalation through tense bird lips, the quick white flash of a turning page. Another exhalation, another page. Exhalation, page, exhalation, page.

I tried to send my mind away from the bathroom, imagining the dazzling projectiles of light that might be soaring over our heads, imagining how strange they would look caught like stars in someone's eyes, imagining myself running down long passages of empty streets. I told myself that even if I couldn't do this, even if I couldn't flee and roam at will, then there must somewhere be a creature who could. A creature untethered who knew the face of time, who knew how to find the way out.

Inside my gas mask, my breath was hot and sour; I could taste the onions I had eaten with my dinner and the chocolate milk I had for dessert. Inside my mask, the world was too silent. I remember thinking – exhalation, page, exhalation, page, exhalation, page – that this silence reminded me of swimming in the sea, of diving under the waves and letting my body go limp, pushing out all my air so I could sink to the sandy bottom.

My mother told me later that I slumped over, knocked my forehead on the lip of the toilet, and crumpled onto my side. She said that she was scared at first, panicked even, but then she had realized I was just being melodramatic. When I asked my father about it, he said that he didn't remember it happening at all.

What I recall is the coming to, the slow resumption of living. There was no sense of speed, no sense of moving upward toward the light, there was only the sense of having been somewhere else for a time and now returning. When I woke, my gas mask had slipped off my head. Gone was the taste of old onions and chocolate milk. No more air-raid sirens, either. I was on my back next to the toilet and, for some time, I just gazed up at the underside of its white porcelain. Eventually, when watery light from the hallway began to filter in, I realized that the bathroom door was wide open. The sun was rising, and someone must have opened a window because currents of fresh air were flooding into the flat. I took a deep breath and smelled the warm salty stench of the sea.

52 Days

When I wake, I am afraid that I am someone else. I see a handprint on my wall and a print of another kind on my floor. I yearn for water, a lake of water, to drink and drink until my belly splits and spills great fonts of blue from my innards.

When I wake, I go to my mirror trailing sweaty sheets and I startle myself. I remember the dreams that I had when I was young, when I feared my whole life would slip away from me while I slept.

When I wake, I remember the places in which I have recognized the way out: in the black pupil of a stray dog's eye the moment before it was hit by a taxi and its skull skittered like a cracked egg on the street; in the soft pink of a fresh burn on the inside of my mother's thigh the exact size and shape of a smoldering cigarette; the street outside Escape Now after the first winter rain when the asphalt goes black again for the first time in three seasons and we walk, marveling, across something brand new.

When I wake, I hear sirens and I go to my window.

When I wake, I stumble to the bathroom mirror and find that there is no witness.

When I wake, I am sure someone else is staring back at me.

51 Days

Mostly, the men are young, not much older than me, in button-down shirts and shiny slacks, their black hair pomaded in oil slicks that pour from their skulls as they flow up the wide stairs, eyes bright and eager. They are missing their families back in India and Bangladesh and Pakistan, but for now they are here and they have money in their pockets and that means cheap tikka and cheaper beer and waitresses to tease. They leave the world behind as they ascend – with every step forgetting crackly phone calls with wives they barely know, forgetting the smell of the bunkroom they share with five other men, even forgetting that they never seem to save enough to pay for everything their family back home needs. Here, in Copper Top Touristic Grill, they live in the bright lights of the future they bought with loans and long employment contracts, this future that means, back home, their photographs hang in pride of place. They are Gulf Men now.

I sit at the bar where I can put my back to the room and watch everything that goes on in the mirror behind the bottles. I watch the Filipino waitresses rush in and out of the kitchen door – their smiles like masks snapping onto their faces the moment they emerge. I watch the bouncer with his thick neck and no eyebrows glaring at everyone. I watch the band on stage belting out old songs while they shimmy beneath the flashing lights.

A group of US servicemen come in and fill the table just behind me, ordering mountains of food. The smell of charred beef coated in black lemon floods the air with a sour green scent. The band finishes their song and the men roar. One of them claps too fiercely and his elbow hits a beer bottle, sending it to the floor where it smashes. The men cheer again. The man who crashed the bottle to the floor is handsome, or ugly, I cannot tell which because his face is a stage of ceaseless drama, with a booming smile, and eyes that stretch saucer-wide when he laughs. Even sitting down his body lumbers like something from a distant prairie past of Conestoga wagons and campfires. Looking at him, I imagine the carcasses of animals, useful beasts slaughtered and gutted and skinned.

When the waitress appears with a broom to sweep up the shattered bottle, Conestoga tips her, sliding a crumple of bills into the front pocket of her apron, and calls her 'darling'. When she leaves, he looks up and sees me in the mirror staring.

He bellies up to the bar next to me. His dark eyes are somber. 'What happened to your face?'

Still watching him in the mirror, I tell him that I fell down.

'Looks like someone hit you.'

'The doctor said it was a miracle my head didn't split open. Like the monkey.'

'The monkey?'

'In the yellow smock. With the diaper.'

'What?'

He smells like clay, earthy and pliable. He is big, his vast shoulders stretch the sleeves of his shirt in a way that looks uncomfortable. I wonder if he is uncomfortable. I wonder if that is a thing you can ask a stranger: how does being in the world feel to you? Do you wish it felt differently?

'Where you from?' he asks. 'American, right?'

I consider what answer I can give him that will satisfy us both. Instead of responding, I turn away from his reflection and look at him in real life. I decide to smile. He smiles back and asks me if I want another drink. I say yes. I want to drink the bar dry and at the end of the night I want to pour myself down the street and slosh my way into whatever bed will have me.

He clinks his bottle into mine when it comes: 'Here's to not having your head split open like the monkey.'

The beer makes my throat sting and my eyes water. I finish half the bottle in one go, letting my breath leak out of my nose until I'm desperate for air, which makes Conestoga smile.

I was wrong about him. As we talk, I learn that he isn't in the military, though he used to be. Says that he liked seeing the world and he misses the camaraderie of it. Now, though, he builds buildings all over the Gulf and mostly lives out of a suitcase.

As we drink our way through several beers, he keeps looking over my shoulder toward the entrance, waiting for a friend who he says might not even show. Conestoga explains that his friend, an artist who does installations, has been brought in for the mural project in the souq to commemorate the new millennium. The idea of it, he explains, is to cover the sides of buildings with trompe-l'œil murals that reflect on the past and the present as a way of honoring where we've been and where we are going. He rolls his eyes as he says it, like the whole thing is a joke. He says his artist friend is mad – in the way that means crazy, he clarifies – that he will do anything, no matter how ridiculous. He has three passports, so he can go anywhere, and he never says no.

'And he's getting a kick out of the hoax. Thinks it's hilarious that so many people fell for it.'

'Hoax?'

'The new god. Didn't you hear that the archeologist who made the "new god" discovery has stopped giving interviews? People are saying he made it all up.'

'Made up the past?'

'Well, if you can convince enough people to believe you it just becomes fact.'

'But why?'

'Maybe he's crazy, too. Spending all your time like that, with your head in graves and shit, you're bound to lose it.'

The band announces they are taking a short break. There are boos and catcalls, and then the sound system kicks in with a bouncy pop melody. Through the haze of smoke and flashing lights, I watch Conestoga finish another beer. When he winks at me, it doesn't quite work, his left eye stutters in the making of it. He lights another cigarette even though he already has one smoldering in the ashtray next to him.

'Are you sure your friend is real?' I ask.

He gives me a blurry smile. 'I swear he said he would try to stop by. He's just busy, can't ever stick to a schedule. You know how it is.'

'How do you know he really exists?'

He leans into me. 'You're kind of cute when you're trying to be funny.'

I let him lean into me, let my body take on the weight of his shoulder against mine, and tell myself that I can hold up the both of us. There are things I want to do to his body, but I can't yet tell exactly what they are. I imagine long fingers piercing the skin of his chest, finding his heart. The pulpy wet give of it.

'What would you do,' I say, 'if one day you realized you'd made your friend up? And that all the facts you knew about him, his job, the way he takes his coffee, the kind of women he goes for, all of it was dreamed up by you?'

Conestoga leans back and exhales a cloud of cigarette smoke. 'I don't know. I guess I'd think I'd lost my mind.'

I erase the distance between us and press myself into him, feeling his body sway under the sudden pressure. 'And what would you do if you realized that you'd made him up in your head…but he was here anyway. Real. Walking the streets.'

He belches softly. 'Fuck, I don't know. That's weird.'

'What would you do?'

'If I made some guy up in my head only he came true somehow? Like I dreamed him up and then he was standing there in front of me?'

'Tell me what you would do.'

'Fuck. I guess I'd kill him. I'd have to, right? He'd be an abomination.'

I lean back. 'Kill him?'

He scrubs a hand across his mouth. 'You sure your head isn't fucked up from falling down?'

Then he laughs and tells me I shouldn't be so serious all the time.

'Smile, darling,' he says, trying to give me another wink. 'It can't be that bad.'

I tell him that I think it might be much worse than either of us knows.

He says he has to take a leak and he tells me not to move while he's gone. He pokes me on the shoulder like he's dotting the end of a sentence and then works his way through the room, knocking into tables, slapping friends on the back, leaning heavily on the banister as he goes up the stairs.

I wait for a minute, and then I follow.

At the top of the stairs there is a narrow hallway with water stains on the threadbare carpet. The music from down below is quiet, like I have traveled a great distance. Overhead, there is a single blinking fluorescent light that has a rhythm to it. Flash. Flash. Flash. Dark pause.

I hear a toilet flush and then, emerging from a door on my right, Conestoga appears, zipping up his jeans. Over his shoulder, I catch sight of urinals, cracked floor tiles, and a busted mirror.

Seeing me, Conestoga's eyes fill with a sticky sort of wonder. He thinks I have followed him up here. I *have* followed him up here.

His face comes into focus, sharpening.

I step back and my heel knocks into the wall.

He speaks a slur of misshapen vowels.

I turn for the stairs.

He grabs me.

The sharp bite of fingers on wrist.

Time bloats, catching everything in a pocket of stillness so large that I am able to revel in the details of the scene we are making between us. As Conestoga's face closes in on mine, as the pressure of his fingers on my wrist increases, I can study the rims of his eyelids, the curious portals from which the pale hairs of his eyelashes emerge. The curl of his asymmetrical nostrils. The faint scar winding over his top lip. The give of his wide stomach pressing into mine.

He raises his free hand.

I flinch.

But then softness.

His fingers rill my brow bone, my cheek bone, my throat.

His breath spreads like a curtain of fog against my mouth.

And then my wrist explodes in pain.

He tears at me, twisting my arm up above my head, and his thighs crush into my pelvis. My head smacks into the wall and the teeth behind my eyes snap to life.

Within the trap of his arms, I am still; I offer no resistance because there is no one here to resist. I have always known that I am nothing but an empty street roaring with wind, and so I have no reason to mind when

Conestoga's mouth buries mine within its wetness, or when he bends my wrist so far back that buzzing insects swarm my skull. The things that happen to this body have already happened to this body and will always be happening to this body. There is only ever now.

A shout. A female voice. Conestoga drops my wrist and steps back. On the stage-set of his face, anger, betrayal, like I have done something wrong. He mutters words that I don't catch and then he is gone, making his way unsteadily down the stairs.

I turn.

At the end of the hall is an open door. As I move toward it, I can hear the buzzing blink of the light struggling over my head. Three swollen crescendos and then a brief ditch of silence. I wait through three more of these cycles, three orbits in this space, three circuits of time, before I step through.

The smell of laundry soap and toothpaste. The smell of too much cigarette smoke in a too small room. The sight of a ceiling fan draped with undergarments – a black bra, a white bra, a purple bra. Five sets of bunkbeds running down each wall, three dressers beneath a row of narrow windows.

There are women lounging in their beds, one writing in a notebook, some dozing. Off-duty waitresses. There are hair scrunchies piled on side tables, pantyhose hung over bed railings, and an open box of tampons on the windowsill. And stuck to the wall beside every pillow are small photographs of children.

A woman near the windows is ironing a white shirt. She glances up, meets my eye, and says, 'You don't belong here.'

50 Days

I wake to soft gusts of rain filling the world. No red planet tonight, only a fragile wash of blue and grey across my apartment walls. The sound of car tires in puddles, the muffled rumble of thunder, the watery call to prayer.

I roll my wrist to discover what is left in my bones from last night and find that there is a dull deep ache, as if Conestoga's fingers are still upon me. The phone rings. I think it rang on and off all day as I slept; I can remember tendrils of this noise finding its way into my dreams. I think of the putty-pink envelope still lurking beneath my bed and I wonder if the two are connected, paper and noise, handwriting and ringing.

I get up and say, 'Hello.' First to the empty air in my flat, hello to the nothingness, but then I say hello into the handset.

There is a quick cough at the other end and for a moment it *is* the putty-pink letter, the raspy smoker's cough that I know so well, the girlish ducking of the head.

But then a man's voice. Officer Bayan. He coughs as he talks, the two running into each other, speech and gargling exhalations.

'A witness?' I ask. How can there be a witness to the hit-and-run now, after all this time?

He will not answer. He just says that he needs to speak to me. He has been calling all day. Can I come into the station tomorrow?

Into the silence he coughs again and something from the depths of his lungs works free. He excuses himself, asks me, around a mouthful of this something, if I will hold the line. I imagine him reaching across his desk for a tissue, I imagine blood coming from places where it is not meant to come from.

I wonder what Officer Bayan would say if I told him about Al Ghareeb, who cannot be real and is walking these streets. Or the letter beneath my bed and the woman in the painting with the doomsday breasts. Or Malak with her visions of the end, and Conestoga with his friend who is mad in the way that means crazy.

I hang up before Officer Bayan can return to the phone, then I vomit into the toilet. My mother would never have allowed this when I was a child. She said toilets were filthy and that, while gagging, the body would suck up new particles of sickness and grow even sicker. Things can grow in the blood that can take over the body, she always told me, things that we don't even know are there. She made me throw up into buckets and wastebaskets, she made me throw up until my eyes were pouring and snot streamed from my face, saying 'better out than in' while stroking my back with her long fingers.

After, I rinse my mouth out in the bathroom sink, and I catch sight of my reflection. There is a flare, on the right side, a sliver of protruding collarbone that is higher today than it was before. I think of shifting landscapes, the rising heft of mountain ranges belting up like knuckles from the skin of the earth. When I meet my own gaze, I cannot discern the viewer and the subject. I get back into bed and ignore the ringing phone. I blink my eyes a thousand times until the fringe of muscles behind my face throb. I jab at the most painful point of my jaw, desperate to bring back the hot filaments of pain that had appeared right after the accident. I terrorize my body, waiting to feel once more like the empty street that I am.

But in this new rain-scented day I understand that my emptiness has been violated. I knew it last night when Conestoga was shaping himself around my body, and I knew it weeks ago in the moments just before I stepped off the curb and into the screaming onrush of headlights. The empty street has an intruder. I cannot feel it always, but I know it is there: something large and unwieldy, something massive and furious. This is why when I awoke in the emergency room I scrambled my hands over my body, trying to find where I had been breached. I imagined scraps of skin, splinters of bone, passages opening where passages should never open.

Now, in my rain-washed room amid the sound of a wet and gleaming city, I rub my legs against the soft cotton of my dirty sheets. They itch where the road rash is healing. With my nails, I begin to scratch. Clumps of scabs come away beneath my fingernails, gooey black flecks that I flick across the room or swipe onto my pillow. Looking down, I see that the scabs have left behind strips of skin that are taut and shiny pink. In the weeks since the accident my body has made a newness that did not exist before.

Something is coming.

49 Days

The souq is dazzling with water. There is the fresh dark smell of rain and the moon's reflection swimming in puddles.

Everything is washed and novel, even the shop windows are clean and clear. Across from the archeological site at the end of my street, I see newly erected scaffolding and an array of paint cans and rollers. Conestoga's mad friend must have surfaced. I wonder what vision he will bring before us.

There is the smell of cardamom tea boiling out of a tea shop and I can see four kittens pouncing in an overturned trash can. A tailor has positioned a mannequin wearing a Santa suit in his doorway, draping his shoulders with cotton wool to give the illusion of snow. Over the doorway, shiny tinsel letters spell out *Happy Christmas!* A taxi slows to a crawl at the curb in front of me and the driver rolls down his window, thinking I'm looking for a lift. He smiles when I wave him away, teasing me, saying no lady should walk alone in the rain. I shake my head and he drives off.

And there, across the street, is Al Ghareeb.

In the fine haze, his helter-skelter eyes watch me.

My body floods with the blood of a thousand hearts and, for a moment, the two of us just stand there staring at one another. An hour or a month or a year passes and then a shoulder slams into my back and I stumble forward.

When I right myself, Al Ghareeb is gone. The street is thick with people tonight, men walking hand in hand, women carrying bags of laundry, children throwing rocks at fat pigeons. When I spot him again, he is moving away from me, walking toward the bare stretch of coral stone wall that will soon hold a mural. I watch him say something to the man standing beneath the tarp with the paints. And the man replies.

So, now I know that I am not the only one who can see him: I have brought him forth and now he exists for everyone. My abomination.

I use my elbows to push my way through the crowd. A little girl riding her father's shoulders blocks my view, lifting her arms up to sway her torso, left right, left right. I step into the street to go around them and a horn bellows. I jump back onto the pavement just in time to miss being hit by a school shuttle. Its wheels kick up a dingy spray of water that splatters my legs.

I catch sight of Al Ghareeb turning the corner, but, when I get there, I find only Green Jack standing all alone in a misty halo, his body shot through with falling moonlight, his paving-stone face pure.

'It's all coming to an end,' he says, his voice thrumming like the engine of the world. 'Think now on the tawdry tomorrows we are free of. Think on these storms of grief we will escape. Think that the end might be a door, a window, a cloud with all of its breath removed. The end might be the way out – think!'

Al Ghareeb is crossing the street now, wending his way through the slow creep of traffic. He isn't running and he isn't looking over his shoulder. Perhaps he does not even know I am following him. Or perhaps he knows that I am following him and he doesn't care. He enters a cold store, and a bell dings over his head as the door swings shut behind him.

I lean against a watch shop window across the alley and wait, staggered by the idea of my abomination in a shop, perusing aisles of fish cakes and soda and soap. The banality of it is a horror. I wonder if I will speak to him – if I *can* speak to him. What his voice, made of rocks and tide water and grief would sound like?

He's not been inside long when he emerges carrying a can of Vimto. Against the loud purple logo, I see that his hands don't look the same as they did the first night I saw him. His fingers look sharper, even less human than before. All of him is a warning – the sickly pale skin, the body that is too tall, the dense spray of unkempt hair. And the eyes. More than anything else, it is the eyes that mean danger.

He opens the can and drinks it dry in long, steady swallows. When he is done, he crushes the can in his hand, and I wait for him to toss it in the gutter, but he finds an overflowing dumpster and places it atop the rubbish and watches to make sure it stays put.

I follow him down Kitab Avenue where the popping lights dazzle my vision and the smell of roasting meat turns my stomach. We turn left and pass the swampy-green froth of Al Hadiqa, and on the next block we weave through a child's birthday party, dodging children with sticky hands and bobbing balloons. A chicken truck has overturned at the intersection, white feathers and squawking birds in dented cages fill the road, and Al Ghareeb slips down an alley.

Into the darkness. My feet slap the slick asphalt, sharp sharp sharp against the empty tunnel of coral stone walls. Everything is unravelling. I'm not going forward, but down, toward the center of the earth where all things are birthed and cut loose. I leap over a broken door on the pavement. A crunching field of shattered glass. Already far ahead of me, Al Ghareeb turns out of the passage, and I go faster.

I round the pile of rubbish at the end of the alley and realize too late where he has brought me, where I have allowed myself to be led. The encroaching scent of the sea should have been warning enough. The tall white-and-blue flanks of the Milk Milk building soar upward into the stringy clouds, and, in the abandoned playground next to the building, I see the broken slide beside the busted frame of the merry-go-round. Half of the seesaw is missing and the monkey bars have been hacked to bits. Out of habit, I glance up to the third floor, wondering if, in the flat facing the sea that I know so well, my absence has even been felt.

Al Ghareeb moves slowly, thoughtfully, through the brush and rubble of the abandoned playground. From the mouth of the alley, I watch him step over the broken slide as if it were nothing at all and I imagine – *I see* – the harsh gleam of hooves. Approaching the tall side wall of the Milk Milk building, he bends his head back at an impossible angle to take it in. The paint is peeling, has been peeling for years. I fight the urge to run out and shield the wall behind my body. Nothing should be looked at the way he is looking at that building.

For a long time, all he does is stare. I count the seconds and lose track at two hundred. I tell myself time is not real and I can wait here forever because I am always waiting here forever.

I shift on my feet, a slight nothing of a movement, but it must have been enough because Al Ghareeb's head whips around and his wild eyes pour toward me. He takes three quick steps in my direction, drizzle dashing off his shoulders, and I tell myself that I will face him. I tell myself I will step out of this alley and find out why he has come. But then I see the play of his fishbone fingers, white against white, and I stay cowering in the alley.

And then I see he was not looking at me at all, but at the Pyramid that stands at the far end of the Milk Milk building. Ten feet high, made of dense dusky-green hedge that was long ago trained around a cone of splintery wood and chicken wire, the pyramid is hollow inside. I still remember the damp living smell of its interior, the gnarled roots, the fragile web of leaves at the very center. The Pyramid was where we played when we were young, several of us crowding our bodies inside at once. We brought candy and sticks and dolls made of twine. We told jokes and we told stories. Sometimes Malak predicted the future. The Pyramid is where I first said the name Al Ghareeb aloud, where I first described his shambling nocturnal walk out of the ocean, his lonely search for home.

Al Ghareeb closes in on the Pyramid. I strain to see him, leaning halfway out of the safety of my alley, wiping rain off my face with my sleeve. He lifts his long arms and plunges his hands into the green tangle of the hedge. Deeper and deeper he goes until he is up to his elbows in it, until it looks like he is forcing himself into the foliage, as if he will take one more step and be gone – then he begins to tear.

Unhurried and seemingly unbothered by the vicious thorns that I know exist within the dense shrubbery, Al Ghareeb slowly pulls down the entire hedge. He works methodically, bracing his back and yanking strenuously when a particular stretch of hedge resists his work. When he is finished, the mangled remains of the Pyramid lie at his feet. It looks like a small pile of nothing.

Al Ghareeb then reaches into his pocket and pulls out something that is too small for me to see. And, with a smooth, sweeping motion of his arm, he lunges forward. Within moments there is light leaping along the ground, flames are chewing up the Pyramid's remains, illuminating his silhouette from beneath. Tall and thin, sharp from crown to heel, he stands surveying his work. Here, in this world of mist and water, Al Ghareeb has conjured flame.

48 Days

There is a man made of rocks living on the streets and I can hear his steps. The rhythm is off, the way he walks is wrong, it is a stagger, a bone-deep stagger, the whole of his body falling too heavy and wrong on the earth. I can hear the sloppy reel in his hooves. I rise up from dreams singed with ash, dreams charred with spinning eyes, thinking of the ache still in my wrist.

Someone is knocking on my door. The footsteps are a fist. The fist is here, the sound a pummeling in my skull. Something is wrong with my leg, my back. Every day when I sleep the accident happens again and every night when I wake my body knows the moment it met the street. The fist on my door is made of rocks; the accident in my body is right now. A voice shouts, 'Hello.' In his burning, Al Ghareeb pulled himself that much further out of his watery tide and into the real world, and, in his wake, things are shifting.

I am asleep, dreaming of the carcass, and then I am awake dreaming of the carcass. The Pyramid in the dirt with the sharpness of his body leering tall over the death of it. The flames eating it to nothing. I need to see it.

The sun has set, the streets are chaos, the noise of the people and the cars and the cats and the wind pass directly into my bloodstream, and I feel myself swelling with pressure. I fill the streets that I travel, I torment the corners, my body a bloated current of troubles. All the way to the Milk Milk building I can smell the sea, the wild lie of it, everything exposed.

Into the playground across the gritty soil, I look for the prints of cloven hooves, but the ground is too trampled, too irregular and rough for anything to show clearly. Over the broken spine of the slide and around the ravaged monkey bars, the smell of burning joins the smell of the sea, and there it is: a small heap of burnt nothing. Every green leaf is gone, just a few of the thicker root stalks remain, curled and clenched like fists groping at the soil. The beams of wood are carbonized, bones gone black, only the chicken wire still looks as it once was. Pieces of it gleam through the piles of ash, silver and winking like shards of the moon.

Last night, I cowered in the alley while Al Ghareeb stood like a column of faultless white in the black smoke and watched it burn. When the flames sputtered and died, he turned and walked away, back onto the streets, leaving me behind. Now, I stand where he stood, in the same place, looking down at the Pyramid's carcass. I sift through the ash, bringing up a handful to rub into my face. Conestoga said an imaginary being brought to life would be an abomination. I push a heel into a limb of charred dirt and I wonder if this is what he meant. This small and needless death.

Without the Pyramid the Milk Milk building is totally exposed and it looks cold and vacant, like a body without its skin. Looking back down to the charred ruin at my feet, something warm and wet drops against the rim of my upper lip. I reach up to wipe it away and find a smear of red on my finger.

The taste of blood is the taste of time. I open my mouth and use my tongue to pull it in. The taste of iron and nitrogen and hydrogen cast out billions of years ago in the death throes of an ancient star. Salt and heat and somehow the taste of soil rich with the turnings of new life. There are eons in my blood. Something was knocked loose in me the night of the accident, but not from the impact of the fender or the crash into the pavement. It was knocked loose in the moments before I stepped off the curb, when a new world burst to life within me, exploding and exploding and exploding.

=

It was Eid, not long after the war had finished, and we were leaving the souq. My father was driving, and my mother was in the passenger seat, occasionally rolling down her window to smoke. When the cool autumn air snuck into our car, it tangled my hair and filled the space with the scent of woodsmoke and rain. In the backseat, I kept my forehead pressed to the window, watching as one by one the cluttered buildings of the souq fell away. Without them leaning over me, the world seemed like a place where anything could happen. When we got to the sea road, I kept my gaze fixed on the bulb of the sun as it fell into the water – even then I had trouble keeping my gaze on the slouching malevolence of the waves. The war had finished, but I kept imagining a man who could emerge from the tides.

We drove on, leaving behind all signs of the city. We slipped through the palm farms, shopping malls, and spacious compounds of the suburbs; we passed through narrow villages whose streets were crisscrossed with holiday bunting and filled with families gathered around platters of yellow rice and roasted chicken. When we breached the colossal emptiness of the open desert, the music on the radio began to catch and blur with static. My father switched it off and we drove on in silence through the vast fields of burial mounds where we were the only car on the road. Thousands of ancient gravesites spread out around us on either side, stretching toward an invisible horizon and taking on curious shapes that looked like clusters of crouching men or wild horses with too many heads. Overhead, the sky was thick with stars.

Consulting his compass and map, my father eventually brought the car to a slow crawl and bumped us off the road entirely. Skirting wadis and rounding jebels, we made our way into a desert darkness that seemed to carry on forever, as if the whole world had disappeared. I asked when we would know we were getting close, but neither of my parents answered, they were both squinting with concentration into the illumination given off by the headlights. I turned around to look where we had come from, but there was nothing to see: no lights, no village, no city at all. If something happened to us out here, I wondered how long it would take for help to arrive.

'Watch out!' my mother shrieked as my father hit the brakes. My body lurched forward and my face knocked into the back of the front seat.

Sitting back, I saw a small goat with floppy black ears and luminous yellow eyes blinking in the glare of our headlights. Her mouth hung open, revealing the tidy white pillars of her perfect teeth. She was lost, separated from her herd, distant from the safety of a farm. My father leaned on the horn to make her scurry away, and we drove on.

Cresting a steep rise, we saw it: a red and black tent perched behind a roaring campfire. To the left was a hulking generator, out of which ran strands of twinkling lights. To the right, two jeeps modified for the desert with running lights and fat tires. In front of the tent a short man, shorter even than my father, was coming out to meet us.

We got out of our car and greetings were made. First my father and Saeed clasped hands and kissed, exchanged pleasantries, asking again and again after the other. And then Saeed's wife, Yasmin, emerged – a tall, graceful woman with a round figure – along with two other families and a sprawling mass of children, some lurking with dolls, others kicking a soccer ball in darting figures around the campfire.

Food was served immediately. Roasted lamb, curried potatoes, rice, salad, hummus, goblets of juice, boiled eggs, and fresh bread. We ate sitting on a Persian rug, digging into the food with our hands. The oldest of the children sat to my right, and I noticed as he ate that a slick of grease formed across the top of his lip, like a fine mustache. When he caught me looking, he whispered that he had brought something cool for us to do later, something that would really freak out the parents.

The younger children were antsy, and they got up often from their seats to run outside and jab sticks into the campfire. They complained that they were bored of their day in the desert, that they wanted to go back to their homes in the city, where they had movies to watch and video games to play. Hearing this, their parents pulled them into their laps and fed them bits of meat and rice, or squeezed their cheeks. I watched with a sense of unease as the parents laughed, wiped smudgy faces, and ran fingers through tangled hair. It looked like a performance, like we were being lied to.

Throughout dinner, Saeed told stories in a barrage of Arabic and English that made my father tilt his head back and laugh, showing the backsides of his yellow teeth. This was a thing I did not often see, and so I watched carefully this new and different man, this novelty in the shape of my father.

Saeed called to me in the middle of another story: 'When we were your age, your baba spent more time in the desert than the schoolroom. Did you know that? He still speaks better Arabic than I do. There's steel in his tongue, wallahi, steel. And he knew more about the Bedu than anyone. He read all the books, knew all the stories. He knew how to walk like them, find water like them, even how to hunt like them.'

Hunt? I couldn't imagine my father hunting – not the man I saw in his small office with the mess of papers and red pens, sagging ferns and wayward clocks.

Saeed nodded. 'He rigged wire traps and always got his prey. He knew every time where to find whatever it was he wanted. Hare, snake, even dhub! You know dhub? Your father could catch a dhub faster than anyone I knew.'

Coffee was poured and the adults continued to talk while the children ran out to fling dates into the campfire. I lingered in the doorway of the tent, watching them run and shriek. The oldest boy, the mustache of grease on his upper lip gone, went to the bigger of the two jeeps and began to rummage in the back. He emerged carrying a small paper sack. The other children, seeing it, began to whisper and point, then followed him at a respectful distance. When he stepped up to the edge of the fire, which roared and spat sparks into the black sky, the flames made me think of wild tendrils of hair, electric and moving.

The first noise was a gunshot. Stepping on its heels came a storm of explosions, one after another, so quick and so sharp that my ears felt torn from my skull. I screamed and fell to the ground clutching my head. Miniature stars leapt free from the fire, sparking and skittering across the sand. One of them landed in the hood of a little girl's jumper. She howled in pain.

Even when the noise of the fireworks the boy had chucked into the fire stopped, the bedlam continued inside of me, the explosions trapped in the envelope of space between skull and brain, a shred of space too small to contain so much. I was on my knees in the cold, damp sand and everyone was staring. When I felt the hot sticky wetness running out of my nose and down my face, I began to sob. It ran hot and thick down my chin and into my open gasping mouth. I sputtered and wet came out.

'Your shirt, you idiot, don't ruin your new shirt!' my mother cried, running out of the tent with a wad of tissue in her hand. She pushed me around the campfire, through the gawking children, and into the backseat of our car, pressing the tissue against my nose. It smelled of her powdery perfume, and the grip of her fingers was punishing. We sat in the back seat for long minutes, my mother holding the tissue, me trying not to cry. When she finally pulled the tissue away and still blood poured from my face, she cursed and shouted for my father, telling him we had to leave.

From the darkness of the backseat, I watched him and Saeed emerge from the tent. Saeed said something to the boy who had tossed the fireworks into the fire, which made the boy drop his head and scuff a heel into the dark sand. But when my father came out, he rubbed a hand across the boy's shoulder, and said something that made him lift his head and smile.

We drove slowly back through the desert, the car lurching over dunes, my nose still bleeding, but more slowly now, filling tissue after tissue with a steady creep of blood. My mother kept turning around to frown at me, to check my pupils, to lay a hand on my forehead to look for fever. She asked me repeatedly if a firecracker had struck me, if some debris from the fire had smacked me in the skull. She checked my pulse while watching her wristwatch, and told my father that it wasn't right, that something was going very wrong.

My father did not speak. Not even when my mother asked if he could drive more quickly or when she said she would send a note of apology to Saeed and Yasmin, along with some halwa, or maybe chocolates. He just squinted into the headlights as we drove on through the desert toward the distant highway.

But then he began looking at me. Not often, but with a regularity that I could not predict. There was no preparing for the flicker of his blank gaze settling on me in the rearview mirror. I knew it wasn't all that would happen. I waited for him to look at me in the mirror and then shout, threaten, tell me what an embarrassment I was. It was coming. It always did. He was peeling me apart like he was peeling apart the desert, his gaze like the headlights pushing me further and further into the darkness.

'I hate you.' My words came out slurred with blood and something else that might have been the clotted weight of the black night pressing into the car on all sides.

My voice was quiet, but it grew louder. And louder still. A stream of words, a jumbled rush of rage and battering anger, louder and louder, until I had my fingers clenched so deeply into my own palms that I felt blood coming from there, too. I screamed at the back of his head, I screamed at his vacant eyes in the mirror boring into mine, I screamed at the cold empty night in this world where anything could happen.

And then there was a small, terrible sound. It was already gone by the time I registered it. Something must have happened to the wheels.

We stopped. And looked. We had hit something.

'Stay put,' my mother said, her voice sharp, but I leapt from the car and ran.

The body we found was even smaller dead than it had been alive. Crumpled to nothing on the edge of the road was the goat with the floppy ears and the luminous yellow eyes. The skin of her head had been peeled away, the red meat of her exposed.

My father nudged the body with his toe and the goat's little mouth fell open, revealing the faultless white rows of her teeth. 'Do you see what you've done?'

The drive home was silent, save for the rain that began when we reached the palm groves of the suburbs. In the soft hiss of it I thought of other worlds where things were different. My father had taught me the theory of the multiverse, saying that physics all but proved that multiple dimensions existed and that in them every possible permutation of reality played out. There was a world where I had never been born, a world where I was born to different parents, a world where the war had never come, worlds upon worlds where everything was true.

As the wheels of our car slushed through puddles and the city slowly regrew around us, I thought of a world where my nose had not bled, where I had not screamed, where my father had not had a reason to stare at me in the mirror, and where we had not run over the lost goat. A world where she was still alive.

My nose finally stopped bleeding when we were very close to home. I gathered up all of the tissues that had gone hard with my dried blood and clenched them in my fists. I thought of everything I had let escape my body that night and the repercussions this world had meted out in return. I thought of a body without its skin, a smallness of blood and eyes and teeth.

47 Days

I walk for hours through the heart of the souq, avoiding the pull of the Milk Milk building, wondering what has happened to the world. I dreamed a dream and the dream has come to life. He has led me to the womb of his own myth and burned it to the ground. Where is he now? Is he there, in that cold store, buying another can of Vimto? Or in the passenger seat of that sedan rolling down a too-small alley? Where in this tangled body of cement and asphalt is he lurking? He is behind every black window, hiding in every shadow, the souq is filled with his specter. I can feel his fishbone fingers plying the molecules of air at the nape of my neck and I can hear the clatter of his hooves on every corner. I wonder if a dream can be unmade.

46 Days

'—never found the body—'

'When? A baby?'

'—told you, I haven't seen anyone who looks like that.'

'Three dozen oysters and a single white rose.'

'—all over the place, she just kept screaming, said it felt like—'

'Already gone, exit-only visa.'

'Somehow, he did. Fire on everything, just ate him up, like when—'

'—don't have to respect her, you can do whatever—'

'Didn't you hear the sirens?'

'I said I haven't. You sound nuts, you know that?'

'—you mention it, maybe I have. Let me think. Red hair? By the bank yesterday—'

'—strange, isn't it? Very strange.'

'Fuck hope. That's a good start.'

'—stop it. No one knows where to go.'

'Would you leave me alone already? What is your problem?'

'—said he was already gone. Yes, exit-only. Who knows. Who cares?'

'—already the best price, wallah, you won't find better. Take it now or else.'

'Can I go? I need to go. I have to get out of here. I really have to get out of here.'

'—like a goat? Listen to you! The things that come out—'

'The juice of two limes and a pinch of saffron.'

'I never saw anything like that. Astagfirallah. Be quiet.'

'Yes, right into traffic. Wallah.'

'The Milk Milk building? Isn't that where you grew up?'

'—yes, a hoax, exactly. Because he's unstable. He'll do anything for the attention.'

'She used to be somebody. Not somebody important, but somebody.'

'—lies. Everyone wants to die.'

'Not two hours ago, just down at the corner.'

'They're covering all the walls in murals. We live in some sort of story now.'

'Well, how should I know? Burned is burned.'

'No skin at all, I'm telling you. And the teeth—'

'—please? Please? Please? Please!'

'If you go fast, you might catch him. What do you mean, he's not real?'

'—he's already dead somewhere, they've just got to find the body. Right?'

'She stepped off the curb and then it was over.'

45 Days

Mrs Al Jabri is waiting at my front door. I've come up all of the steps toward my flat, through the blinking lights and the on/off existence, only to find my way barred by her squat figure and slipper-bound feet. They are red and white, like candy canes. Last Christmas, Mrs Al Jabri's front door was wrapped like a glossy green gift with a big red bow over the peep hole. She asked me if I liked it, if it made me feel merry, because you were supposed to feel merry this time of year. I told her no, it made me feel nervous because she couldn't see out. 'How will you know who's waiting for you on the other side,' I said. She had laughed like I was telling a joke.

And now here she is, breathing heavily, tapping her slippered foot in front of my flat.

'What do you want?' I ask.

She shakes her head and lifts her hands, emitting a whine as thin as the whistle of a tea kettle. 'You will be the death of me, wallah, the death!' She thumps a fist against her chest. She does not move to let me at my door. 'The police are after you, girl, the police! And you have them coming to my building where everyone can see. The death of me, the death!'

Just the sight of uniforms in the lobby, coming up the cramped and dirty staircase, would have every tenant in Mrs Al Jabri's shabby building peeking out of their doors to see who had done what. Mrs Al Jabri lives on the top floor, with the best views, and almost never leaves her flat. The police would have had to travel up many flights of stairs, and pass through many periods of nonexistence, to speak with her.

I tell her I will talk to them. I explain that it isn't something I've done, that it has to do with the accident.

She squints at me, her eyebrows knuckling down over her eyes. 'What accident?'

It has never occurred to me that she didn't know. Everyone knows. It is the souq; everyone knows everything. 'The accident. The doctor said it was a miracle...' I trail off, wondering if I should bring up the monkey.

'Oh, that,' she waves a hand, and for a second I think she's about to push me down the stairs. 'That happened long ago. No, they want you for something new, I'm sure of it. Something you've done. Wallah, this will be the death of me.'

As she makes her way up the stairs, I watch her, even while trying to remember how long it has been since the accident. I consider the marks on my leg. Partly scabs, partly newly forming scars, they don't look very old. They look as though they are fresh, like every day they are remade.

44 Days

After the rain, the streets are washed and new, and the buildings in their huddled crowds gleam. A dense foam of jasmine pours over the Post Office balcony, and from every window box at the money exchange comes an exhalation of white bougainvillea. Coming out of Goody

Hypermarket I see Malak carrying a sack of groceries. When she sees me, she smiles, her small face a spotlight of brilliance in the middle of the crowd. I ask after her mother. She has rallied, apparently. Her lungs are clearing, her memory returning. Maybe she will live all the way until the end.

On the next street I see Abdullah and Liam smoking shisha on Sinjin's balcony. They shout down to me that Sinjin has lost his job, after all.

'Where will he go?' I shout back.

They shrug and blow smoke rings over their heads, and ask me if I have seen Caleb. I ask who is Caleb, I don't know a Caleb, and they look at one another and laugh.

'He knows you,' they shout.

From another balcony there is the sound of an argument, someone is screaming in a language I don't recognize. Turning onto Madkhal Avenue I find a revelation of blue. The side of an office block, three stories high, is drenched a potent blue. The color repudiates the night, inviting the eye to imagine a dimension where buildings are the midday sky, where sunlight hits the atmosphere between every molecule of cement.

There are men in jumpsuits smoking beneath a rampart of scaffolding, squatting on paint cans, looking over their equipment. These are the mural makers. I cannot tell what this blue vista will be when they are finished; for now, it is only a field of indigo, the deepest part of the sky, the very bottom of the sea. Standing in front of it, I feel myself falling, if I could just let go of whatever it is that holds me to this life I would be gone.

The lower left corner of the blue vista splits, spitting out light, and a man emerges from the open door. I watch him leave his strange dimension of color and make for the street. It's his walk that I recognize, the generous, loping quality of it, like a saluki, the lithe dogs of the desert who run down wild hare in the fiercest heat. He has clipped his hair much shorter than it was in the photograph that ran in the paper, but his beard is still long, a thundercloud hanging from his chin. In the years since I last saw him in person, he has changed. He looks older than I know he is and his eyes are pouched with shadow.

I watch him enter the antiques store with the painting of the nude with the doomsday nipples in the window. A moment later the shopkeeper is pulling that painting from the display, leaving behind an easel that now sits empty beneath the overhead spotlight. When the archeologist leaves a minute later, he is carrying the painting, wrapped in brown paper, under his arm.

It is easy to slip into the crowd behind him. People are rowdy tonight, drunk, there is noise and movement to hide myself within. I tell myself I will follow the archeologist to the cemetery but no farther, he will turn east and I will let him go. But when we get to the cemetery, he does not turn east, he goes to the rusty gate in the stone wall beneath the jacaranda tree and shoves it open. It gives way with a jagged screech and he does not bother shutting it. I follow him into the field of the dead.

There are no crowds here for me to hide behind, so I go slowly, hanging back, watching him wind his way down the dirt paths, around the lines of rough gravel that conceal the bodies, each of them facing toward Mecca. There are no gravestones, just small pillars of gathered rocks and a few clumps of windblown flowers laid here and there. From the distant street comes the cry of a siren.

When Elias reaches the northern gate, he pauses. I wait beneath the canopy of a tree and watch him shift the painting in his arms. It is framed in heavy wood and is cumbersome; it has been a struggle for him to carry it this far. He looks winded and I wonder if he is sick, if something has happened to him. I think of the newspapers, the tourists, the people whispering about a hoax.

I am unprepared for him to turn around and face me, and when he does my body cringes as if I am about to be struck.

'So. You are real.'

This is the first time I have ever heard his voice.

'I was beginning to think you did not really exist, going this long without us ever meeting,' he continues, taking a step toward me. 'Were you planning on following me all night?'

'I was just walking.' My voice comes out loud, tense. There is a ringing in my ears. Suddenly, I am aware of all the dark places in the cemetery, all the spaces where things could hide.

'And when you saw me, you thought you would tail me. Where did you imagine I was going?'

Over the years, I have imagined any number of things about Elias and his life. I used to walk by the water chamber site when he first arrived, as if I could learn about him that way. At times, I longed to meet him, and at other times, I hated him, but it was like hating a natural disaster — it felt futile even as I did it, like screaming at a tidal wave. My father never talked about him, never mentioned my mother leaving at all. But standing here now with Elias in the graveyard, on the same narrow path, surrounded by dead bodies, is something I never imagined.

'People are saying that your new god is a hoax. They're saying you made it all up.'

His eyebrows lift, he is surprised this is what I'm speaking to him about. I have the feeling that, over the years, he too has imagined a conversation between us many times and I wonder how he thought it would go.

He inhales deeply, considering his response. 'It isn't a new god, though. No one should have ever called it that, I certainly didn't. Something four thousand years old is hardly new.'

'If it's a hoax, does it matter?'

He doesn't answer. In my tone there are traces of that old anger. Still, he watches me, so I watch him. I think of Al Ghareeb and I wonder if he is out there among the quiet graves watching. If an old god can be born again, what of dreams? I wonder if Elias would understand that kind of question.

'Why did you buy it?' I ask, nodding at the painting in his arms. 'It's one of her worst pieces. She hated it, you know. I remember her saying that she sold it just to get it out of the house so she wouldn't have to look at it anymore. She won't be happy about you bringing it home.'

He hesitates, his eyes troubled. 'Have you not heard from her?'

I think of the putty-pink envelope living beneath my bed and I don't know how to answer. I shake my head but say 'yes' at the same time, both responses jumbling within me.

'Ah,' he says. Ah, as if he understands, and, standing here in this cemetery that smells of mud, I think that maybe he does.

'Look, if you really do want to speak to me about the old god, come by the site. The sign out front says "no visitors" but the gate isn't locked. Just come in and tell the guard that I'm expecting you. You can see everything for yourself.'

He turns and pushes open the cemetery gate. This one does not screech, it slides open easily, shifting a hanging tree branch, which rains down blue flowers. And then he walks away without looking back.

43 Days

The rain seeps into my dreams and everything spins with the motion of it. My mind is pushed apart by the sense that I am in two places at once: in my bed asleep and also standing outside my apartment building, rain running into my eyes. I am watching for something, but I don't know what. I feel new in the world, tangled and embryonic, still tethered to other streets beneath a different sky. Everything is distance, everything is falling down.

When I wake with my heart on my tongue, everything sweat-slick, I tell myself I will not look for him tonight because things that are not real cannot be found. I grind my face into my mattress until sparks flare behind my eyelids, till my lips on my teeth are tender with pain, till my nose is crumpled and I cannot breathe. Al Ghareeb is not real, of course he is not real, and that means that things are, once again, going very wrong. There is a dizzying moment when I realize that looking backward to my past and looking forward to my future are the same. It is all an unraveling.

Onto the street. The reek of fresh paint from a nascent mural. *43 Days* reads the apocalypse clock. Little boy with a cigar in his mouth. Old woman shouting from a rooftop. The sheen from a tower of black cherries. The smell of ash and oud and jasmine and raw meat. Two cars have met in a collision, fenders crumpled, and a taxi driver is rubbing his bloody chin. Red blood on white thobe. A cat with something hanging out of it. Three crows in a cage screaming.

In the antiques store where the doomsday nipples once lived, I find that the tour guide is now the shopkeeper. He is still shaggy and morose, still sad at the eye and grim at the jaw. 'My cousin owns the store,' he explains. 'And sometimes I help out.' He looks embarrassed or guilty, I cannot decide which. I ask if he has any more paintings by the artist who did the nude that had been in the window.

He tilts his head to one side. He thinks they might have a few. Coming out from behind the counter, he moves toward the back of the shop and tells me to follow.

'The artist you're looking for did a whole series of paintings about the souq years ago, which are still popular, especially with tourists.' He grunts as he cinches in his waist to move through a narrow section of shelves. 'When we get one of those, we sell it quickly, so if that's what you're looking for…'

'No. It's her later work I'm interested in,' I say, squeezing through the same gap.

We come to an intersection. To our left, are giant mirrors surrounded by gaudy frames; to our right, are shelves of figurines, brass camels and wooden dhows. We turn left.

'She's an expat, you know. I think from Canada or maybe France, but her family has lived here a long time, something like a hundred years.'

America, and seventy-one, I correct him silently.

In the lane of mirrors, he catches my eye in a reflection and winks.

'If you buy something tonight, I will charge you extra. For what you did.'

'For what I did?' A lifetime of depravities comes to mind.

He laughs like I already know what he is going to say, as if we have had this conversation many times before. 'The tour? I saw you slip in when we were at the house site. You looked bored and you didn't stay with us long.'

I ask him if he knows the archeologist.

'Elias? Sure. I worked for him for a while when he first came over to start on the water chamber site. He has strange ideas, you know.'

'About the new god?'

The tour guide shakes his head. 'Even before that. I never knew who he would be from day to day. Some days good, easy. Some days he was like a monster.'

'An abomination?'

The tour guide laughs. 'Exactly. That's exactly right. He could work all day and all night, and he expected us to do the same. He has these theories about the past, about how, if we don't get to it quickly enough, it might change on us. He was always saying that his work was a race against the clock. But the things we found, they'd been in the earth for thousands of years. Could they not wait a little longer?'

We reach the rear of the shop where a mahogany cabinet holds antique compasses and clocks, some tarnished, some gleaming. I notice one with a crumpled metal lid where it looks like it was hit by a bullet, and another with a minute hand sweeping around the face twice as fast as it should.

'Well, these are what we have,' the tour guide says, running his finger along a stack of paintings leaning against the wall.

Working my way through them, I see that most of the paintings are from a transitory stage in her career as an artist, between her souq period and self-portrait period, when she painted portraits of others and domestic still-life scenes. These were never popular; there is an awkward stiltedness to them and the color is flat, like an afterthought. I remember her saying that during this time she felt like she didn't paint anything at all, that the paintings would appear, finished, on her easel and she would sell them for what she could get, not remembering the making of them.

In the center of the stack, between a study of a street cat and a portrait of an elderly woman, I find a painting of a drab living room, and pull it free from the others. It is a scene of emptiness. In a small room a seaweed-green sofa sits in a chunky square of sunlight that adds illumination but somehow leeches warmth. There is a murky sideboard in the background topped with a smudge of dull grey paint that does not resolve itself clearly, but that I know is an antique snuffbox of mahogany and silver. I remember that it smelled like a slice of subterranean earth.

'I'll take this one.'

The tour guide is too good an occasional shopkeeper to show surprise that I want this not very good painting. He praises me for my keen eye and carries the work to the front counter where he begins to wrap it in newspaper.

'Wait,' I tell him. 'Not yet.'

I hand over a fistful of bills, which are still damp from being in my rain-soaked jeans. After pocketing my change, I pull out my knife. Flicking it open, I bend to the painting and use the sharp edge of the blade to work the canvas free from the frame. It goes quickly. The tour guide, startled, asks me what I am doing, but I don't answer. Quickly, I shake the canvas free and, holding it in my hands, flip it over.

This other painting is almost identical to the first: same drab living room, same murky sideboard, same smudgy snuffbox sitting in the cold sunlight. The only difference is that in this hidden painting, perched along the back of the seaweed-green sofa, there is a figure. A young girl, hunched at the shoulder and uneasy in the hands. Her face is tilted awkwardly to capture the light and her features are unsettled, they clash and work against one another.

'Oh,' the tour guide says. 'Is that…'

'Yes. When I was young. Eleven, twelve maybe.'

'The eyes…' he says.

'…they're all wrong,' I say.

=

When I was young, my mother would dress me in fussy dresses, brush my hair so hard I cried, and take me to galleries where waiters carried silver trays of fish eggs on toast and the sound of popping champagne corks made me wince.

'Look,' she would say, 'look at the walls. That is my work up there. That is me.'

I would wait in the corner, watching her move through

the crowd. She was all sharp angles and light. A wide mouth, hair a curtain of pale blonde, and her dark eyes set slightly too far apart so that she looked startled, as if the world was forever alarming her. She smelled of her paints. Always. Of linseed oil and white spirit. And there were splotches of color, vermillion or indigo, speckling her wrists.

Her work was beautiful then, image after image of the souq's streets, an endless, sunlit city of narrow alleys and brilliant skies. She had a way of catching movement without rendering too many distracting details, implying with only a few strokes of her paintbrush everything she wanted the viewer to see. It was the souq perfected; there were no dead rats in the gutters, no men spitting on the pavement, no rubbish and no smog. All was clean and glowing, antiseptic and sterile. Modernity was nowhere to be seen: no cars, no shop windows filled with televisions, no digital clocks counting down to the apocalypse.

But, during the war, she stopped painting and spent her days and most of her nights in the living room watching news on the television. She pulled out an atlas and used the heavy silver snuffbox to hold it open to the page that showed a map of the Gulf. Sometimes I saw her write things in pencil in the margins of the map, but they were always erased before I could read them. In my memory, she didn't eat a thing for the entire duration of the war – it seemed she survived on cigarettes and karak chai, nothing more. She even stopped cooking, which meant I spent a few days eating dry cereal and crackers before my father saw what was happening and brought home sacks of frozen ready meals, which I could cook for myself in the microwave. The thinner she got, the wider her eyes appeared, the fringe of her pale lashes lying like spiderwebs across her pink skin, as if at any moment something might come crawling across them.

Late one night, I found her sitting on the floor in front of the television, her knees up to her chin, her arms wrapped around her legs. She wore a white nightgown with a high collar that made her look like a little girl, and in the ashtray next to her a cigarette had burned away so that it was nothing but a long pillar of ash. The news was showing a reporter, wearing a flak jacket and a helmet, standing atop a hill of rubble that he said used to be a school. There was a long winding streak of dust on the reporter's face and as he talked a bead of sweat, falling from his forehead, carved a path through it.

My mother turned her face toward me and I watched as the light from the television drained off half of her skin. She watched me without blinking. 'If you died, I would die.' She said it quietly, her voice gentle as a cloth falling to the floor. 'If one of these bombs gets you, it would have to get me too.'

When she turned back to the television, I went back to bed where I lay awake for the rest of the night, waiting to hear the air raid sirens, wondering if I was going to die and if I did how my mother would make sure that she died too. I imagined the ways she could then take her own life, the pills she might swallow, or the knives she could use on her wrists. I wondered if there were other ways that I didn't know about yet, simpler and quicker methods that would give her the same way out. I told myself that must be love and I let the word settle like a stone in the pit of my stomach. I imagined it covered in moss at the bottom of the sea, an ancient unwieldy thing.

When the war finished and she began painting again, her style was different. Not gradually, but instantly. There were no more scenes of a perfected souq, now, only portraits. She painted everyone. Our maid, her friends, the neighbors, even people she met on the street and convinced to come upstairs and sit for an hour. She offered them juice and cookies, and told them again and again to act natural, to just be themselves. The perfection was gone, too; these portraits were vividly realistic. When she painted the wart on our neighbor Um Bader's chin too exactly, Um Bader told my mother she was a harpy and stopped inviting her to tea.

She painted me only once. It happened in the weeks after we killed the lost goat. Things had been wrong ever since that night – more wrong even than before, and in ways that I didn't understand. My father hadn't spoken to me since we returned from the desert, not even when I made a few faltering attempts to speak to him. I even apologized once, one night when we passed each other in the hallway. I said, 'I'm sorry,' but he kept on walking, checking his wristwatch as if he had some place to be.

And then there was the lock on the outside of my bedroom door – a small slash of silver metal that made a slick noise when clicked shut. My parents installed it the morning after the night in the desert, my mother explaining that it was because of my frightening rage, my terrible fury, she called it, shaking her head sadly. Watching my father work the screwdriver into the flimsy door, she said there was no telling what I might do.

The morning my mother painted me, I had spent hours locked in my room. I had backtalked, said something ugly to her as she was unpacking groceries, and I had been hustled into my bedroom and the door locked behind me. Slick and sharp the small sound. I thought of hooves striking pavement. For a few hours I sat on my bed, reading, looking at the ceiling, staring out the window at the sea three stories down. I told myself I could stay in my bedroom forever, that being locked inside was not really very bad. Along the horizon I imagined the sea was churning, that something was happening somewhere far down below. I waited to witness it.

When my mother came back to unlock the door she stuck her head inside, her white-blonde hair falling down beside her face. She said I could leave my bedroom if I asked for her forgiveness and promised to sit still while she painted me. I asked for her forgivingness and made the promise.

She positioned me on the green couch in the living room and spent a long time arranging the curtains so they would let in a generous amount of light. It was early afternoon but winter, so the light was clear and so bright that it made my eyes hurt. I didn't know what to do with my body; it had never occurred to me that my mother might want to paint me and I felt unprepared. She folded my hands in my lap and tucked my heels against the back of the couch. At the sight of my hair, she shook her head and pushed it behind my shoulders to conceal as much of it as possible. Being so close to her, as she stood there with her hands on my body, made me tremble. There was a newness to her smell that I had never noticed before – beneath the cigarettes, beneath the oil paints and linseed oil, there was a wash of gummy sweetness, like something going rotten.

In silence, she began to paint. The scruff of brush on canvas, the soft sound of paint being squeezed out of tubes, the muted pop of her lips on the end of a cigarette. The world was rich with fragments of sound, and with her eyes, the roving thrill of them as they skated across my body.

When she finally spoke, her voice was rough, as if she had just been woken up. 'All I ever wanted was to be a mother. Did you know that? To have a family of my own. But people don't tell you what can happen. All the things that can happen. Children ruin things you aren't prepared to be ruined. You give everything, but you get nothing back. That can destroy a person.'

She put her paintbrush down and stepped away from the canvas, assessing. Her hair lifted in the current of air coming from the AC, and a strand of it drifted across her face, catching at the corner of her mouth. She left it there as she continued.

'I make sure to give you the life I never had, and maybe that's the problem. Everyone says that you're spoiled, you know, that I do too much. But I just didn't want you to want for anything like I did when I was your age. I just wish you knew how lucky you are.'

She told me to stop fidgeting, to look back into the light, and then she picked up her paintbrush again. My neck was beginning to ache from holding myself in the position she had insisted upon and I wanted to speak but didn't know what I could say. I wondered if I should apologize again, if I had done something else wrong, something that I didn't even know about. We lapsed into another silence, listening to the afternoon prayer call and the voices of the pigeons conversing on our window ledge. I was about to ask for a break so I could move my neck and stretch my legs when she began to speak again.

'You know, your grandmother went crazy once.'

She said this easily, like she was remarking on the weather or the curry she wanted to make for dinner. Her shoulder even lifted, half a shrug. I thought of her mother, who lived in a pink seashell of a bungalow in a beach town in Florida. Her husband, my grandfather, lived in a rambling nursing home nearby. We almost never visited and when we did my mother became a strange, feral creature, spending the days pacing on the veranda or going for long drives by herself.

I met my grandfather only once. We went to his nursing home, which was composed of endless lemon-scented hallways and small paintings of gentle meadows on every wall. I wondered if they were all the same meadow and, if they were, whether the dimpled hills were a real place somewhere in the world.

'Hi, Dad,' my mother said when we entered his room. There was a window that looked out onto a parking lot ringed in billboards. Against the white sheets of the bed my grandfather's body was mottled, purple and brown, with liver spots, and he seemed too small to be an adult, too small to have lived an entire life. With a grunt he lifted up his narrow head and I could see that his eyes were the same as my mother's, the wild bigness of them, the eternal surprise.

He twitched a finger and told her to sit next to him on the bed.

She settled on the edge of an armchair in the center of the room. I lingered in the doorway and listened as they made small talk, as if he was not her father, as if they had never even met. Her voice galloped through her sentences, telling him about the flight over, the changes in the souq, the thunderstorm that woke us up that morning.

When he noticed me in the doorway, he lifted a hand, reaching for me, and I went to him, arms open, but my mother snatched the back of my shirt to stop me. She pulled me toward her and perched me against her hip on the edge of the chair. I could not remember the last time she had held me like this, but she kept her arm tight around my waist for the rest of our short conversation.

When my mother, behind her canvas, told me in her matter-of-fact way that my grandmother had gone crazy, I decided I could see it. Living in her small beach house, visiting her frail purple husband, dealing with the infrequent visits of her strangely furious daughter – I could picture the unraveling of her mind.

I said this to my mother and she looked up, a single line creasing her wide forehead.

'What? No, not Mama. Your *father's* mother. *She* went crazy once.'

This I could not imagine. My father's parents' house, in a manicured gated subdivision, was a place of rigid angles and gleaming hardwood floors. Every time I spoke aloud in that house it seemed to cause a minor shock, like I had said something vulgar. My grandparents' lives ran like clockwork – as far as I could tell, they kept the same schedule every day, waking early, going for a walk, getting groceries, preparing meals, watching their television programs. There was no room for going crazy; all the time they had was already allotted for other things, meted out and carefully guarded.

During our rare visits my father was quiet, quieter even than he usually was, sometimes so quiet I could forget he was there at all. He would sit in corners, taking up as little room as possible, saying only, 'Yes, sir' or 'No, sir,' when his father spoke to him. Whenever his mother tried to hug him, I noticed that he would always clutch her shoulders warily, as if he might break her, and keep his eyes tightly shut.

'Really?' I asked my mother now, being careful to not change the angle of my head as I spoke. The light from the window had shifted across the room as she painted, and now that it was pouring into my eyes, everything shimmered.

'Your father was young when it happened. Younger than you. Your grandmother was shipped off to the States for treatment – electroshock. That's how it was back then, and your father had to watch over himself. His father was too busy working to keep a close eye on him.'

My mother frowns and leans in toward the canvas, does something fiddly with the edge of her brush. She works at whatever it is for a long time before she is satisfied, before the frown leaves her face and she begins speaking once more.

'The thing is, when your grandmother finally came back home, she was different. They had done something to her memory and, at first, she didn't even remember your father's name. He was like a stranger to her.' She switched to another paintbrush. I saw a small daub of white at its tip.

'But what did she do?' I asked. 'I mean, how did she go crazy?'

'The way people always go crazy,' my mother answered. There were, she said, the half-lived days that my grandmother sleepwalked through, the way she locked herself in the bathroom to pick out every strand of hair in her eyebrows until she emerged looking as smooth and red as a scalded chicken, and the people she saw on the street who weren't really there. There was a vast emptiness within her, my mother said, and she simply fell into it.

Then my mother put down her paintbrush and wiped her hands on her smock. 'You need to know what could be in store for you, is what I'm trying to tell you. What's in your blood. You had better learn to control yourself because there is no telling what you could be capable of.'

My mother rolled the stiffness out of her shoulders and called me over to look at what she had done. Standing at her side, I looked at the painting of the sofa, the cold sunlight, and me. The colors she had used were muddy and jarring – ochre and beige and sawdust grey – and in the painting I had her too-long neck, my father's marble head, and in my lap my hands were a crude tangle. My body looked unfinished, like something misplaced.

Picking up a small brush with a narrow point, my mother dabbed at the painting and sighed. 'It's your eyes I still can't get right. They're all wrong.'

42 Days

I wake to my own face watching me. Eyes that float and tremble, colors that loom. The painting is propped up against the wall across the room from my bed, and I know it has been watching me all day as I slept. The eyes that float and quiver are still all wrong, my mother never succeeded in getting them right, but the fingers are finished, they are beige sticks broken against one another, clutching at nothing.

I sit up and stare at myself staring at me, and decide that I feel good about this situation. Waking to your own self is a positive thing, I think, knowing that you haven't dropped your guard even while sleeping. I tell myself that I will not go crazy again, that all of this stops now. The Stranger is a disturbance and I will not look for him because he is not real. From the street I hear shouts in Tagalog and I tell myself that I am hungry.

I go to Larvad's and order vegetable cutlets with black onion seed gravy. I'm the only woman in the place and Larvad's is so small there is no family section for me to hide myself in, so I sit at the counter and ignore the stares. I feel like a lit fuse.

Larvad cooks my order fast, wanting to get me out before someone sees me alone in here and rumors swirl about the kind of restaurant he runs. Plopping peeled potatoes into his big pot, he rips out burps with no shame and tells me he gets gassy whenever there is a shamal. Tells me this one is going to be bad. Tells me when shamals happen late at night like this you know the whole world is off kilter. He knocks a knuckle on the big steel pot and tells me he carried it from his sister's house in Kochi. Tells me his electricity bill has doubled now that they are charging expats more than locals. Tells me he's not going to buy the good onions anymore, just the cheap ones from the village. Tells me he thinks he has heartburn from eating mango out of season. Tells me Caleb was asking about me. I say I don't know any Caleb.

'Well,' Larvad says, 'he seemed to know you.'

And then Badal comes in at the kitchen door with a cardboard box of onions in his arms, staggering beneath the weight. Larvad whirls on the boy. 'I told you to be quick! Cretin boy, stupid boy, donkey boy!'

Badal unloads the onions as fast as he can, cringing under the torrent of abuse. He is Larvad's cousin, and came over two months ago to work and save up money so he can get married. He was skinny when he arrived, and now he's skinnier. Unloading the onions, he is all sharp hitchy motions, razor elbows, and slicing shoulder blades.

Still tossing out insults – ugly boy! shameful boy! – Larvad tells Badal to go scrub the floor by the front door. He wants the black scuff mark there gone. He wants the floor to shine, to gleam, to tell customers that Larvad's has a floor so clean you could lick his gravy off it and ask for more.

I watch Badal get a rag and a bottle of vinegar and crouch over the scuff mark. He unscrews the cap of the vinegar bottle and soaks the rag. The smell lifts eyebrows across the room. Everyone is watching. The boy attacks the mark. His back bows up, his back hollows down, his legs flex and shake, his head hangs – he's using every part of himself to clean the scuff mark on the floor that has been there for my entire life and is never going to budge.

As Badal is crouched there, heaving his whole body into the work, the bell over the door dings. A customer enters, knocking the door into Badal's head. The customer looks down. Badal looks up and apologizes. I'm sorry. He shakes his head. I'm very sorry. The customer frowns and goes to the counter to place his order. Badal resumes his scrubbing. His ribs bellow, his pelvis thrusts, his legs tremble.

A few minutes later, again the bell dings. Again, the door swings open. Again, it hits Badal. The customer frowns, Badal apologizes. He shakes his head. I'm very sorry. From my stool, I watch this ritual play out many times over the next few minutes. No matter how Badal positions his body, it is not possible for him to avoid being hit by the door. He crouches one way and it gets him on the knee. He crouches another way and it gets him on the backside. Another way and it gets him on the shoulder. And every time, the apology, growing more and more frantic with every telling, as if he could prevent all of this from happening to him if only he were sorry enough.

Larvad catches me watching and rolls his eyes. We are in on this together, he is implying, he and I are a united front against the stupidity of this awful boy. Larvad shouts at Badal to hurry, to go faster, to get it done, but he shouts in English, which Badal doesn't understand.

I could leave. Make a protest of it. But I still haven't gotten my food. Larvad shouts again, and this time some of the other customers laugh and Badal ducks his head. I'm sorry. He shakes his head. I'm very sorry.

I take a sip of my silty tea and give into it. I let myself go flush with Larvad, put myself in alignment with him. I look down at the stupid boy, the shameful boy, and I feel the great distance between the two of us. It feels good. All of this feels good. I think of my father reading his book as the air raid sirens wailed during the war, and I think of the way he drove his car over the body of the little goat in the desert without swerving or even touching the brakes. The vision is pure.

41 Days

At Pearl Good Electro there is a windowful of televisions that are each playing a different movie. *Pretty Woman*. *Star Wars*. *Mughal-E-Azam*. *Sholay*. *Rambo*. *Mother India*. *Alice in Wonderland*. *Fantasia*. *Gol Maal*. *Men at Work*. *Swing Kids*. *Anand*. *Guide*. *The Bodyguard*. *The Breakfast Club*. *Made in America*. And still others I don't recognize. The screens are a jumble of flashing lights and motion; I expect the actors from one to leak over into the others. Permutations on permutations. I am waiting for all the worlds to bleed into one.

40 Days

On the way home from work, I take a shortcut down a black alley, and my leg encounters a soft warm flash. It is there and then it is gone. I spin around, my eyes swallowing up the shadows trying to see something within them. There. Yellow eyes blink and roll behind a rotting palm tree. It is a cat. I kneel down. The thing is ragged and unwell with scabs on its face and a dead distance in the eyes. I hold out a hand and it bolts. When I stand up again, I feel dizzy. At home, the painting greets me when I walk in the door, the wrong eyes wondering where I have been. In my dreams the feeling of being watched. In my dreams the feeling of watching.

39 Days

The cat in the alley with the dead yellow eyes. She keeps thinking of it. Of the connection they made, the event between them that began with a soft flash of fur on her leg and which is possibly still going on. She is thinking of where the cat had been before, the snatched scraps of rotting food, the litters born sick and small. The bloody fights with other sick cats. The other sick cats scratching and biting. Bites from unclean teeth coated in saliva. The cat's warm slip past bare ankle. The porosity of skin. The induction of disease. She considers her leg and the blood within it. The things it could be carrying.

At the end of her bed, the painting has shifted: the collarbone is higher, the eyes are beginning to slip. The body is taking a different path.

38 Days

I spend time in the bathroom watching myself in the mirror. My skin feels hot. I wonder if disease could take hold that quickly. I wonder what disease it could be. My skin feels hot. When I think of cat teeth I think of rabies. A swiftness in the bloodstream bringing certain death. My cheeks burn and there is a taste in my mouth that I do not recognize. My skin feels hot. My jaw still aches if I poke it hard enough, and, when I do, the sparklers that flare in my vision make me even more dizzy than I was before. My skin feels hot. I think about cutting into my skin, getting knives, sharp things, jabbing through the striations of red and white and pink. I remember the feeling I had in the emergency room, the feeling of having blown apart. Every door in every world flung open.

37 Days

Explosions at my door. A ricochet of noise and motion. I sit up, look at the painting, and think that she has emerged, that her changing body has finally found a way to crawl into this permutation.

But it is not the painting. It is Mrs Al Jabri at the door. I'm killing her. She swears, wallah, wallah, I am the death of her, I am a bad girl.

I think of the moment when I stood before a wall of traffic not knowing there were eyes upon me and I wonder who it is that has gone to the police. There was a moment just before the accident, a fine vein of time, when I knew something was coming.

I must go see Officer Bayan, I must, or Mrs Al Jabri says she will kick me out. She has been good to me, given me cheap rent when she didn't have to, when everyone told her I was majnoona and she shouldn't take the risk, and now here I am killing her. You bad girl, she says, shuffling off on her slow feet, you very bad girl.

36 Days

I know exactly where I am because I always know exactly where I am. Always I feel the streets radiating out like spokes from my body, everything happening to them is happening to me. I am porous, borderless, and sensation floods in that I am powerless to stop. I know it all. I know the world. I know that right this minute at the Shri Krishna temple there are children punching through the milling flock of half-tamed pigeons, sending the birds up into the air, borne aloft on the lift of their beating wings. Sitting beneath the canopy of the temple's banyan tree, I know the children's parents scold and complain, passing bags of pumpkin seeds, saying how much better children behaved back when they were young, back when people had manners, back when the world made sense. I know the taxis creeping in front of the Madkhal, with their drivers who balance paper cups of karak on their knee and honk and honk. I know the ruffle of desert wind coursing along the rooftops, stirring sheets hung out to dry by maids and mothers and big sisters and aunties. I know the rustle of doves in their courtyard coops shuffling their soft feathers, hushing one another to sleep for the long sad night. I know the creeping cadence of cats on their angel paws, prowling the grimy darkness. I know the drift of the moon, the rush of the sea, the dreams of the archeological site full of splintery bones and collapsed skulls and ancient teeth scattered like stars across the sand. I know the lights along Kitab Avenue are still popping on and on, guiding people into the future and into the past, lighting up revelations on this, the night of the world, when everything is happening in the same long-echoing instant.

35 Days

I wake to something trying to escape my body. I am sick in the toilet and then my bowels run. In the mirror, I see a trickle of dried blood caked around the rim of my reflection's left nostril. Reaching my hand up, I wonder if there will be blood on me too. I think of teeth and saliva and sick cats gone dead in the eyes. The weight of memory decanting off a canvas, the body caught in time leaning forward.

I fall out onto the street. I walk toward the house site and I see the shopkeeper's cousin who is now again the tour guide shuttling tourists down the street. They are a flood and he is their master. He nods, curls bouncing over his ears. 'Hello,' he calls, 'hello.' I turn away and walk to Larvad's where, through the window, I see Badal collecting dirty dishes from tables. A skinny man wearing a puffy red parka swats him on the arm. Badal forgot to clear the spoon.

On my leg I feel a warm slip of something living, but when I look down there is nothing there, only the yawning stretch of empty pavement. In the air, I think I smell smoke.

34 Days

The end of the street has become a palm grove with the moon on one side and the sun on the other. We are caught in perpetual twilight. The eye is tricked because it looks so real that I think I could keep walking and find myself in another world, sliding through the brick that now looks like loamy soil and towering green trees.

In the mural's dim shadows that foam up from the soil of the palm grove, there is a cat peeking out from behind a tree. I can feel the warm lick of its fur against my leg. Eyes like lamps. Drab teeth glinting grey. Drab patchy fur rustling with mites. I think of the graves of the burial fields and I wonder what it will be to die. On the corner, a tourist takes a photograph and my head rings with the flash.

'Look, *liebchen*, look at this. How pathetic, how miserly? I need your help, wallah, I need your help.' Greta is in front of me now, pressing up against my body, unzipping her neon green waist pouch to show me a paltry handful of bills and coins. 'This is it. My poor horses. I'm finished, I'm finished.'

I dig in my pockets and give her a few coins, but she doesn't go away. She takes my arm in her hand and drags me down the street. Greta is a five-foot wrinkle of a woman, wearing a psychedelic floral baseball hat that says *Bahama Mama* above the bill, and she pauses her lamentations only to light a new cigarette from the butt of the one she has just finished.

'Um Malak sent me away with nothing. Said she was too busy dying to worry about my horses.'

'But I thought she was doing better? Malak said—'

'Malak lies, she lies! Her mama is going to die and soon. You'd think she'd be feeling a little more generous, but no, no one is and that's going to mean the end of everything for me. All night walking on these poor bones and I have nothing to show for it.'

Greta keeps us moving down the street, throwing her tiny elbows into strangers' ribs whenever we are impeded, and telling me the story of a strange and gruesome sickness that has been sweeping through her stables. Two ponies dead already, a little grey gelding and a fat skewbald mare. The horses might be next – Greta thinks they are starting to show signs of the same illness, and she needs money for vet care and medication. All her lessons are canceled, no one will come to ride because they've all heard rumors of the horses coughing up blood and falling down in fits on the sand. I dig in my pocket and hand her another fistful of coins.

'You're a good girl, like your mother before she ran off, a good girl,' says Greta, who speaks Austrian-accented Arabic and Arabic-accented English. She now spots someone she recognizes across the street and dashes away, jingling her green pouch and shouting their name.

Shop shutters are coming down, the moon is slinking behind clouds, and, upstairs, lights are going out one by one as families lay their bodies down, close their eyes, and vanish into sleep. I watch a procession of small white boats pulled by jeeps come to a stop in front of a fish shop, their hulls glistening with sea water, their shape the shape of a pelican's throat. I feel my fingers bend and sway toward them like seaweed.

Men jump out of the jeeps and into the backs of the

boats, pulling open tubs of salt water where they've stored their live catch. Hauling fat hamour out of the water, they throw the fish to one another in a human chain, into the shop where the fish will be killed and cleaned and thrown on ice to sell tomorrow. And just when I think there couldn't possibly be any more red flaring gills or taut silver muscles straining, there is. Pulled from the warmth of the water into the cold emptiness of the open air, the fish thrash and fight.

I am going home, dragging my tired body along a broken side street, when I see someone I recognize. Framed in the middle of a lane by narrow buildings, there are the wide shoulders and thick neck that remind me of a distant prairie past of slaughtered animals and log cabins: Conestoga. He is walking toward me quickly.

Hide. I need to hide. I look for a place to hide, but my legs have vanished and I cannot move. There is nothing but shallow doorways and shuttered shops, the lane is a slaughterhouse chute funneling him my way.

But then, Conestoga turns into a doorway without noticing me. He lifts a big hand and pounds upon the door before stepping back, clearing his throat, and spitting into the gutter. I feel again his fingers on my wrist, my arm twisted over my head in a shrill maneuver of agony. For a moment, I think I will hurtle my body into his, tear him down, claw at his eyes. I imagine every kind of violence.

When the door opens a field of green light falls out, trapping Conestoga within it. He says something I cannot hear to someone I cannot see and, when the reply comes, his hands close into fists.

In the field of green light, a shadow appears. Conestoga takes a step back and then another. A cloud slips off the moon and in the new brightness I see him, sharp from heel to crown, eyes spinning through every permutation of this hollow night – Al Ghareeb.

Al Ghareeb lifts an arm and points into the darkness at the end of the lane. Conestoga shakes his head. Al Ghareeb steps toward him, but he is so slight compared to the heft of Conestoga that it is like a child stepping toward a cliff. And still he points, nods his head, the wild storm of hair floating about his face. Again, Conestoga shakes his head. He lifts his hands, saying no.

A flash of movement too quick for my eyes to follow, it is light cutting through shadow, a flare, a shout. When time comes right, I see Conestoga on his knees in the street, his head hanging, and Al Ghareeb turning to go back inside. The green field of light snaps out as the door slams shut, leaving Conestoga in darkness.

Getting to his feet, a fallen cliff slowly reconstructing itself, Conestoga raises a hand to his jaw and rubs it. Al Ghareeb has hit him.

33 Days

I am at work with my head in the toilet and everything is finished. I filed the new brochures, refilled the fax machine, and watered the plants. Now there are only a few stray smears of shit left in the deepest part of this white porcelain bowl, which I attack with a sponge and my hands in their rubber gloves. This isn't my job, but when I saw that the janitor had left the toilet bowl filthy, I had not been able to walk away. I think it's been days since I came to work. Maybe weeks. I don't know how much longer it can continue like this without Omar firing me. I already hate the way his eyes will look pained, and the way I know that he'll apologize as if he is the one who has done something wrong. I scrub harder. When the stains are finally gone, I lift my hands out of the water and it is then that I feel it: the squelch of water around my fingertips.

I rush to the sink, yank off the gloves, and scrub my hands in scalding hot water. I count to a hundred. When I'm done, I examine my fingers, the backs of my hands, my palms, and my wrists for any cuts or abrasions. My skin is hot and tender from the heat of the water so it is hard to tell, but I think there is a patch of very red skin beneath the lip of my thumbnail. I probe at it, hold it up to the light, and find that, yes, the skin is permeable there. I can see pinpricks of blood when I pinch this patch. I push at it, squeezing it between two fingers, milking out as much blood as I can conjure, trying to force out whatever germs from the toilet might have slipped in, thinking about all the versions of death that can arise from mistakes like these.

I go to the cleaning cupboard in the hall and pull out the jug of bleach. Back to the sink where I uncap the jug and splash it over my hands. Then my wrists. Then I think about my arms, the soft flesh of my inner elbows, and I splash it there, too. The smell makes my nose burn. This is not just about the red patch beneath my fingernail, but about all of the borders I have left unguarded. All these weeks I have been careless with the wounds from the accident, letting things fester that should never be allowed to fester, and now my body will pay the price. I leave the bleach on my skin for as long as I can stand it, then I clean my arms again with water, soap, water, soap, water, soap, in an endless procession of scrubbing and rinsing. My skin stings and every inch of it is red and flaming, but I don't stop. This is something I should have done long ago.

When I press down on the soap dispenser and nothing comes out, I slump forward, my hands two red claws gripping the sink. I close my eyes and see the path the germs are taking, up the routes of my fingers and wrists, through the boulevards of my arms, into the causeways of heart and brain. I tell myself this isn't happening, but of course it is, just like I told myself Al Ghareeb wasn't real, but of course he is. I knew it when I watched him tear apart the Milk Milk Pyramid and set it on fire. I knew it when I went back the next day and saw the charred husk of it, the leafless stalks of the plant dead on the ground. And I knew it last night, when he hit Conestoga.

I let my hands crumple up against my chest, and I lean forward over the sink till my forehead meets my reflection. There, I lean against myself, wondering how long I have been living in the kind of reality where things like this could happen. Perhaps always there has been a thin point of disintegration between the mind and the world, a soft spot between the bones of the skull where things like Al Ghareeb may emerge.

As the cold of the mirror creeps over the arc of my skull, I remember Conestoga lifting himself off of the pavement. The way he rubbed at his struck jaw. And how, for a moment, I felt a thrill of pleasure.

Like I wanted more.

32 Days

Just before dawn, I tumble into sleep, and in my dreams I am made anew.

31 Days

In dreams she swells through streets like eyeballs blooming from doorways on stalks of regret. She sees a face that is a stage perched atop a wide-open prairie of shoulders. The smell of frangipani and dead moths; drab moon fallen down the pavement. Fallen down the pavement a man made of rocks, violent terrors pulse in his jaw. She would like to strike him, to conjure the clatter of movement that will undo his life. Two locations vibrate on a single string: a collision.

30 Days

I wake up remembering the first time I went all the way mad. The beat of panic in my ears when my parents told me that I had to go to university in America never stopped.

It did not stop when I walked across the stage at my high-school graduation in shoes that left blisters on my heels, and it did not stop when I rode in a swerving taxi to the airport. The panic stayed with me on the three flights it took to get to the States, and it was there when I peered out of my dorm room window at this strange new world I was supposedly from.

There were parties in my residence hall and there was always alcohol, so much alcohol, which I didn't understand because none of us were old enough to drink and it wasn't even allowed on campus. But it was always there: cases of beers, sometimes kegs, and bottles of liquor passed around the overcrowded rooms. Girls would start the night drinking out of straws from fizzy bottles, and end the night vomiting into the bushes in the quad, crying for their friends to hold their hair. Boys were drunk by the time the parties started, their eyes red, their lower lips bulging with chew. They were always asking girls to take walks, putting hands on hips, angling them toward the door. Sometimes when they asked me, I said okay; sometimes I let myself be led.

One night, a boy I recognized from one of my classes, asked me where I was from. He said, 'Someplace over there, right?' He had long blond hair and wore a necklace of white seashells.

I told him where I was from and wondered if he was going to ask me to take a walk. I thought I would say yes, I thought about the way he would feel against me. But then he turned to a friend, smirking. 'Told you,' he said, and I knew they had been talking about me before.

His friend rolled his eyes and they laughed together, but I couldn't follow what was happening. Someone had turned the music up so loud that the windows were shaking, one of the girls dancing in front of the stereo was telling someone else to shut the fuck up, and a skinny boy with dreadlocks was balancing on a chair, working a condom over the smoke detector so people could smoke without setting it off.

'What did you say?' I asked.

'I said, you're full of shit,' the blond boy said, enunciating every word carefully, like I was too stupid to understand him.

I stepped forward, wanting to explain, wanting to figure out what I had done wrong, but I was drunk, more drunk than I realized, and my foot caught on the edge of the rug and I stumbled. Suddenly, I was furious. At the blond boy with the ugly necklace and his giggling friend, at the shrieking girl on the dancefloor, at everyone crowded inside the narrow room that smelled of damp laundry and peanut butter crackers.

'You think you're better than us?' the blond boy continued, shrugging like he was asking a genuine question. 'Is that why you pretend like you aren't American?'

'I *am* American. I'm just not—'

'Yeah, not *from* here. We've heard it. It doesn't make sense.'

'You're either American or you're not,' the blond boy's friend said. 'You think we're stupid or something?'

'She thinks we're stupid and she thinks she's better than us,' the blond boy said. 'Who the fuck has even heard of the country you say you're from? Over there, you ride camels to school? Live in a tent?'

I tried to explain, laying it all out as best I could with the room beginning to spin slowly around me, but they weren't listening. They were getting another drink, watching the girls dance, and lighting cigarettes, even though the boy on the chair with the condom wasn't finished yet.

I barely made it into the dorm's communal bathroom before I was sick. Inside one of the stalls, retching over a toilet, I could hear two girls at the mirror getting ready for their night out – gossiping and laughing. Their voices sounded like they were coming to me from a very great distance. When I had thrown up all I could throw up, I flushed the toilet and, back against the stall door, slid down to the floor. Down there, against the cold tile, the world felt properly contained; I wanted to stay there forever. The two girls at the mirror debated which perfume they should wear and, moments later, the air filled with the scent of flowers and musk. I wanted to ask them for help, but I didn't know what it was that I needed.

The campus was big, I walked it. The road into town was narrow and desolate, I walked it. The town was a bleak expanse of parking lots, strip malls, and gas stations with too much space between all the buildings, I walked it. I told myself that eventually the roar of panic in my bones would settle. But nothing ever settled and eventually I learned it was because time was different in America. Slower. Proof that my father and his books were right. Everything felt the way that a throat feels just before a scream.

In one of my classes, in a lecture hall crowded with students, a professor stood in the remote distance beneath the spotlight of a blackboard and taught that the whole sweep of human history led only to the revelation of emptiness.

'Every civilization,' he intoned, 'every ancient deity, every cherished custom, have all with the passage of time been revealed to be nothing but a momentary flicker of our collective imagination. Is there nothing that lasts? Is there nothing that transcends the vagaries of this world? Or, is there truly no meaning to *any* of this?'

Hands shot up and students began to argue as I slipped out into an afternoon leaden with coming snow. I did not need to wait around for the discussion because I already knew the answer. My father had taught it to me.

Not long after our clock discussion about time, my father had found me in the living room, rapped his knuckles on the old snuffbox, and asked me if I thought it was solid.

'Of course,' I said.

When he picked it up and chucked it toward me, I caught it in my hands, testing the weight of it to know that I was right.

'You're wrong,' he said. 'Can you figure out why?'

I turned the silver box around in my fingers, opening and closing it, while trying to determine my mistake. Finally, I shook my head.

My father settled on the sofa across from me and spent some time smoothing out the creases in his slacks. He was fastidious about nothing but the way he dressed – while his office was cluttered with dirty tea cups and used tissues, his clothes were always spotless.

'Tell me, what are objects made of?'

'Atoms.'

'And what are atoms themselves made of?'

'Protons, electrons, and neutrons.'

'Exactly,' he said. The nucleus, he continued, was at the very center of the atom. It contained protons and neutrons and – he clenched his fists – it was held together by a tremendous force. The electrons, he went on, surround the nucleus in a cloud of probability. He relaxed his hands and let them float up in the air as if they had lost their connection to gravity. I watched them drift and bend, noticing a slight tremor in the fingers of his left hand.

'If one of the atoms that makes up this snuffbox was, say, the size of a football field, we could then imagine its nucleus at the center would be the size of the football down on the pitch.'

He placed the snuffbox on the table and lifted his hands once more to mimic the dance of the electrons. I could see that the tremor was worse in his pointer finger. It twitched toward his palm, quivering, and I realized this was something he could not control. Seeing me notice it, he brought his left hand back down, and settled it firmly against his thigh.

'Which brings us back to the electrons,' he continued. 'The electron cloud skirts the outer edge of the football field like a ring of fog. So, what do you think there is between the nucleus and all those dancing electrons?'

When I didn't respond, my father picked up the snuffbox again and held it so the glow of lamplight flashed off its burnished surface. Instead of watching the box, though, I watched his eyes. All around the irises, I could see white.

'Well, in between the nucleus and the electron cloud,' he said, 'in all of that enormous space, there is nothing but emptiness.'

He handed the box back to me and I held it in my hands like I was holding something for the very first time. I stared down at it, as if I could see all of these vast inner spaces, all of these impossible distances that it somehow contained.

'Even though it is mostly empty space,' he continued, 'it feels solid, like all matter does, because, when you touch it, *your* electrons come close to *its* electrons. And electrons can't occupy the same space. You feel that as resistance, which makes it seem as though things are solid. You can be connected but you will remain, always, separate.'

I was still staring at the snuffbox in my hands but I was no longer thinking of it. I was thinking of my own electrons, my own nuclei, and all of the empty spaces between. I couldn't help but think of how very easy it would be to fall in.

=

The afternoon that I left my college lecture hall I walked so far that I was too exhausted to return to my dorm room, and I slept on a stone bench in a park at the edge of town. When I woke, a wet newspaper had snagged itself around my ankle and there was a web of frost in my hair. That night, I walked again, sleeping for an hour in the bathroom of a fast food restaurant where everything smelled of buttermilk biscuits. When a janitor shouted at me to get out, I stumbled back into the night and kept walking. After that, life was a fugue of constant motion. Sometimes I moved for hours in the darkness never knowing where I was.

One evening, I woke to find a storm in the sky, everything cast in shades of blue and purple. I left my residence hall as the first peals of thunder began to sound and, by the time I walked past the library, rain was lashing my face. I walked for miles, hail battering my skin and skull, leaving me dizzy and shaking. I found myself in the woods that ringed the campus, squelching through wet leaves, crossing icy streams, and using my hands to pull myself up steep banks. I tried to remember the last time I had eaten or had a drink of water or taken a shower. Someone had taken the thread of my life and snipped it. I was falling untethered.

Near dawn, I found myself back at the center of campus. The storm had emptied itself out, there was no more rain, no dark churning clouds, and I stood in the grey glisten of a new day listening to silence. In the gaining light frost on a distant window shone like a field of sky littered with stars. Small and perfect and utterly false.

Then I noticed the ground I was standing on was trampled by a collection of strange marks. They were not like any footprints that I had seen before – they were round and sharp and moved in a lilting pattern that spun and danced.

As I began to follow them, I thought of electrons, of how no two could describe the same pattern or be in the same space at the same time. I turned around and around, walking backward and forward, as the world spiraled loose around me, trying to understand what had happened on this ground where I now stood. When the world slipped and spun so fast that bile seeped up my throat, I knew I was going to be sick. It was only then, when I fell to my knees and grabbed at the onslaught of bare earth with my open hands, that I saw what had become of my legs. In the tilting light of that grey dawn, they appeared to bend backward at the knee, and end in two sharp black hooves.

29 Days

In my dreams, Conestoga's body is a field that is the sky that is the moment I felt his fingers close around my wrist that is the time I stood on a curb before a roar of traffic and birthed another life. I will make from his eyes a glow. He is on a swaybacked mattress in a room that smells of liquor. Old oak dresser and a cheap cotton sheet. On and on this dream, fragments that feel like another life. Eddies of time from elsewhere. Insect eyes slip over the moon and there is big bang static on the television. The press of a cigarette against my tongue. The flick of a lighter.

I wake to sirens. At the window, I find the world in flames. The end has come.

28 Days

Blood. The smell, the heat, the stick of it on my legs and on my sheets. I forgot this was a thing my body could do, keeping time like this somewhere on the inside until it is ready for the deluge. It is a clock that beats irregularly, my period, coming too often or not enough, lasting for two days or two weeks, which I think is a sign of some deep wrongness, a derangement of the tissue. I take myself to the shower.

Last night, when I saw the flames billowing out of a building a few blocks away, I went out onto the street to watch and found Abdullah, Liam, and Sinjin. They were drinking karak and complaining about the firemen who shouted at them to get back.

'I know they have a job to do,' Liam said, 'but do they have to be assholes?'

Sinjin leaned toward me and my reflection tilted wildly in his glasses. 'I lost my job,' he said. 'And I haven't been able to find another.' He then told me he would probably be leaving soon, going back home to Kerala. At this notion, he laughed, a yelp in the night.

We weren't able to get close to the fire because the entire block was cordoned off, making it unclear which building was affected. The gathered crowd was full of theories: one woman standing just behind us, her hair in three grey plaits wound around the top of her skull, said the fire had started on a hot plate. 'They were making noodles!' she shouted to anyone who would listen. The word noodles was loaded, she meant something by it, fury on her scowling face. Another woman pushing a shopping cart loaded down with bags of cat food squeaked by and said no, that wasn't right. 'The fire wasn't a natural fire,' she said, 'but a thing possessed. It moved too fast. Something is going wrong here,' she continued, 'something is going wrong here!' Larvad and Badal were sitting on the curb. Badal, his voice shaking, said he had seen someone carried out of the building on a stretcher and they were wearing an oxygen mask. Larvad told him to shut up and he did. Green Jack was there, too, at the edge of the milling crowd – silent as I had never seen him.

Someone with a mobile phone took a call, listened for

a minute, and then told everyone gathered that the fire was at the Desert Suites building. An old man leaning out of an upstairs balcony shouted down to ask if anyone was dead. The person with the mobile phone said they didn't know. Maybe.

Liam looked at Abdullah. 'Where's Caleb?'

'Don't know,' Abdullah replied.

They looked at me. 'Have you seen him?'

I didn't bother to explain that I didn't know Caleb, I just shook my head and went home. It seemed like the whole souq was filling with smoke, and just standing there on the ground, I somehow felt like I was about to fall.

When I finish my shower, I dig through my bathroom cupboard searching for a tampon or a pad, anything to stem the tide between my legs, but there is nothing. With a wad of toilet roll wedged into my underwear, I go onto the street where I find the air still charred with the stench of last night's fire. A taxi is parked on the curb at the corner with no one inside, all of its doors are open. As I pass, I look in the back seat where I see that I was wrong, there *is* someone in the taxi: a small girl with black ringlets and a bright blue party dress is playing with a doll. When she looks up at me, I see that the doll is a toy monkey, with a stitched bright red mouth, glass button eyes, and a dirty yellow smock. Without taking her eyes off me, the little girl lifts up the monkey and whispers something into its ear.

The first cold store has neither tampons nor pads, nor does the second, so I cross a few streets and circle the dark hulk of Al Hadiqa to check Al Barzakh. The shop keeps odd hours, open sometimes, closed at other times for days on end with no explanation, but tonight I find it blazing with light, its front door propped open with a glittering purple geode. Inside, there is the smell of incense and detergent, the sound of a Bollywood film playing on an old TV, and towering stacks of spices and soda and sweets. There is no one at the till.

On the shelf next to pots of skin bleach cream and soap that promises to restore a woman's virginity, I find a single pack of pads. I clear my throat and say, 'Excuse me,' toward the back of the store.

A door opens and Ismail comes out, squinting, lips peeled back from his pointy teeth. 'We are closed.'

'The lights were on and the door was open.'

'Closed. It's late.'

I put the pads on the counter.

Ismail blinks and nods. Slowly, he crosses to the register, rubbing fists to eyes.

'I've always meant to ask, why the name?'

He asks me what I mean.

'Al Barzakh. Which of the meanings did you mean when you named the shop?'

'I bought the store already named. I just kept it. Maybe the name of an owner before.'

'But it isn't a name,' I explain. I feel like he and I have had this conversation before, maybe many times before, and I can't believe he doesn't remember.

Ismail rings up my pads but the till makes a grim beeping noise and he mutters a curse before smacking it with the open palm of his hand.

'Do you really want these?' he asks.

'Barzakh,' I say, 'is the space between life and the afterlife.'

'Damnit,' he says, smacking the till even harder.

'Or the barrier between salt water and fresh water.'

'It's just a name,' he says, wrestling open the cash drawer.

'But it *isn't* just a name.'

Everything that is happening seems familiar – the way Ismail keeps blinking to clear the sleep from his eyes, the way the geode at the door scatters the street light – it's like I have passed through this permutation before and I understand exactly what will happen next. I lift a hand to steady myself against the counter.

Ismail hands over a portion of my change. 'This is all I have. If you want the rest, take some gum. Or a newspaper.'

I look down at the newspaper shelf and see one with the headline *Souq Fire: One Injured* and I take it. Ismail goes back to the storeroom, yawning.

I open the paper and find an article about the fire at the Desert Suites building that offers scant details, no cause has yet been determined. But there, at the bottom of the page, beneath a caption that reads: *One man, Caleb Lanford, was injured in the blaze. His condition is unknown*, is a small grainy photograph of a face I know: Conestoga.

27 Days

I didn't remember coming home from America. There must have been phone calls and taxis and plane tickets and plane rides and layovers and luggage. There must have been flight attendants and the stink of airplane toilets and turbulence and seatbelts. And there must have been things even before that, because I can, in blurred fragments, recall the bright white interior of a hospital. There was a syringe full of clear fluid that made me sleep and the sleep was a fall that lasted forever and felt like the end.

Once back home in the souq, I found that madness was a constant awareness of meaning. My clean wet brain looked upon a new earth that was ever dawn, where everything was the sulfur white of an infant's skull. I refused to leave my bed, stinking my sheets with the animal reek of sweat. I sensed the streets and felt my new limits, knowing that even if I tried I would be unable to leave the souq.

One day I woke to find my mother swimming into the dim currents of my bedroom. She could only see the feral warp of my new form, but I could see that the threads of her mind, and my father's too, were tied to things too distant to be named. In my restless mind I pitied them both and spoke lovingly of my hooves, how they had the blackness of the space between the planets and the cloven shape of so many tongues. When I was alone again, it seemed I knew new things about the tide and the tilt and the terrain. I knew that somewhere there was a man at the end of a street waiting to speak my name.

My father saw it in me when I was small, and everyone can see it now. The scars winding like rivers on my arms. My eyes that go blink blink blink a thousand times a minute. My hands that are still red from the bleach. The lock my parents put on my bedroom door to keep them safe from whatever it was I might do.

26 Days

'What is your problem?'

This is not the first time the nurse has asked me this question, but I still cannot answer.

'Miss? What is your problem?' Her thick Irish accent flattens with each repetition because she thinks I don't understand her, that maybe I don't speak English. She tries in Arabic. Then she calls over her shoulder for someone named Sandeep to come help her.

I shake my head and leave.

Standing outside the emergency room, I watch an ambulance pull up. The woman they unload is in labor, I think, writhing and wailing. A man follows her inside, carrying a duffel bag. He is wearing shoes that do not match. On the left foot, a black trainer. On the right, a grey house slipper.

When the rain starts up, strangely warm on this cold night, I try again. This time I don't approach the nurse's station – I turn right and find a seat in the women's waiting room where, in the corner, there is a woman who is moaning. Small children tug occasionally on her arm, poke into the potted plants, and peer at the other patients. The moaning woman goes silent and I look at her, expecting something, but all she does is lift her niqab to blow her nose. Her eyes are watery and her face is dusted with russet freckles.

The women's waiting area is sealed off with flimsy blue privacy dividers, each one covered in fliers offering hygiene tips and vaccine reminders. At one corner though, there is a gap that allows me to look out. I can see the Irish nurse behind the counter, on the phone, clicking her pen next to her ear. Every so often there is a swift series of beeps and the big white doors that lead into the treatment area swing open. Through them, I can see curtained treatment bays, nurses in blue scrubs, and doctors in white coats. I wait for a familiar face.

By the time a nurse comes to call the name of the moaning woman, she has stopped moaning. She has, in fact, been silent for some time. Her hands, in black satin gloves, are limp in her lap and her children are scattered in various seats asleep. The nurse says her name three times, he is louder with every repetition but he won't come into the women's section. Finally, the moaning woman lifts her head from the wall and beckons her children to follow. I watch their path to the big white doors and when they open I see the man I am looking for.

He pauses to let them enter the treatment area and then slips out. I stand and leave the women's section, waiting to see where he goes. He says something to the Irish nurse at the reception desk and she nods and begins to look for something in a filing cabinet, telling him she will have it ready in just a minute. He raps his knuckles on the counter and goes into a door marked *Staff Bathroom*. I wait for him just outside. When he emerges, he doesn't look surprised to see me.

'Can I ask you a question?' I say quietly.

Dr Ashguf guides me into a staff room. Inside there are two vending machines and a refrigerator with a child's drawing stuck to it with a magnet. Crayon doctors with grubby eyes grin at me as I sit on the narrow sofa.

'You know, you shouldn't have discharged yourself

against medical advice,' Dr Ashguf says, feeding coins into a machine to get us both a soda.

The drink he hands me is painfully cold. 'You don't understand,' I say, beginning to explain, before realizing that neither do I.

Dr Ashguf cracks open his soda and drinks it dry. His eyes are red and I can see an abrasion on his neck where he has cut himself shaving. When he finishes drinking, he asks me if I have been taking it easy like he told me to, while pulling something out of his pocket.

I watch him remove a small silver cap off what I thought was a pencil to reveal a sharp metal blade. He holds up the little knife but looks at me, waiting for my response. When I nod, he says, 'Good, good,' and then he plunges the blade into his empty soda can.

The sound is bigger than I expected, the sheering slices of metal through metal, and it shifts depending on the direction and speed with which Dr Ashguf carves. He works slowly, pausing often to take stock of what he is making. He asks me why I have come to see him and I force myself to stay sitting next to him on the sofa, instead of running back into the cold night filled with the strange warm rain.

'Is it normal,' I begin, 'after an accident like mine, to… to lose time?'

He frowns into his hands at the shape that is emerging from the soda can. 'Lose time?'

'I think maybe I might be doing things that I don't realize I'm doing.'

He glances at me from beneath his wiry eyebrows. 'What kinds of things?'

'And in the mirror. My reflection. I don't know if it is always me that's standing there looking back.'

He purses his lips and goes back to his carving. The knife screeches as he makes a sharp turn in the metal of the can. 'What does your family think about this?'

'I'm alone.'

'No mother or father? Aunties or cousins?'

I shake my head.

A crease forms between his eyebrows. 'These things wouldn't come from a concussion. You asked if it was normal and the answer is no. I think you should let me admit you tonight, there are a few more tests we can—'

'I can't stay here.'

'If you can't stay here and let us help you, why did you come?'

'I just wanted to know if it was possible. The things I'm talking about. The things happening to me.'

Dr Ashguf sighs. 'Anything is possible, I suppose.'

Permutations on permutations. 'Time is going strange.' I whisper. 'All around me things are happening that don't make any sense.'

Dr Ashguf redoubles his efforts on the can. Watching it, there are times when I think the blade is going to slice into the palm of his hand, but always at the last moment he veers away, sending it in a new direction, changing the shape of what I thought was to come.

When he is finished, I can't understand what he has made. The top of the can has been sliced clean off and the body of it cut to thin ribbons. Putting away his knife, he places the carved can between his palms and lightly crushes it, warping the shape so the ribbons in the middle splay outward. Then he puts it on the table in the center of the room and turns off the overhead light. Taking a box of matches from a drawer near the vending machines, he lights one and drops it in the top of the can, revealing it to be a makeshift lantern. Through the finely cut ribbons of aluminum, the flame flickers, its radiant light dancing out in all directions.

Outside, the warm rain is still falling sharp as nails from the sky. I pull up my collar and look down the street in both directions, wondering which way I should go. When Dr Ashguf told me that he must get back to work, he escorted me back into the lobby and handed me the soda-can sculpture, which was still warm from the match that had only recently burned inside of it. But now, outside in the chill, it is fast growing cold in my hands. Behind me, the hospital doors open and a man in a heavy farwa steps through, his white gutra catching in the wind. When he sees me, he recognizes me and opens his arms.

'My dear, what are you doing here?' He kisses me on both cheeks and holds me by my shoulders to look down at my face. 'Are you alright?'

It is Saeed, the man whose grand desert tent we feasted in during that Eid so many years ago. His beard is dyed very black, but at the roots I can see the hair growing out is grey.

'Alhumdulillah,' I reply. 'How are you?'

'Alhumdulillah. I cannot complain,' he answers, as a car slides up to the curb. Saeed insists his driver takes me home.

Inside, the car smells strongly of the two jasmine air fresheners hanging from the rearview mirror and faintly of cigarette smoke. Saeed says something to the driver in a language I don't catch, and we are off, slipping through the streets of the souq, everything looking far away and fake through the tinted windows.

Saeed, beside me on the back seat, keeps up a constant stream of talk, saying that he just flew in and the flight was delayed and when it finally took off there was so much turbulence that passengers were crying and praying. 'One lady even screamed. I thought we were going to drop out of the sky. No such thing as a good flight, I always say, no such thing. Or maybe all flights that manage to land safely are good flights?' He offers me a piece of nicotine gum, and says that he wishes he never quit smoking, that once you start something you should never give it up.

I am only half paying attention, so strange it is to be ferried through the souq's streets in a car that I am staring out the window at the quickly passing world and thinking of Dr Ashguf's words. Not normal. I wish I had told him more now, told him everything.

We come to a stop at a red light. On the wall to our left is a half-finished mural of what looks like stone-age huts: women tend fires, men lean in doorways, children and dogs gambol. The palm trees in the background are unfinished, their silvery-green fronds float like a botanical cloud above trunks that are still unpainted. I imagine the sound of them, the rustling they would make coasting overhead in the wind.

A slow-moving pedestrian hobbles over the crosswalk with a newspaper over his head to block the rain. The light turns green but the pedestrian is still in front of us. Saeed's driver honks and lifts a hand in frustration.

'What day is it?' Saeed asks me. 'I can never keep track when flying in from Asia. I thought I might have missed a day. Or do you gain one coming from that direction? Anyway, I came straight to the hospital when I landed, but those nurses, battleaxes wallah, those nurses told me

I couldn't see anyone because visiting hours were over. I was just about to call my friend, he's the managing director, you know, but then the nurse, that Irish one, told me the patient isn't even awake. Because of the pain they keep him asleep.' He leans toward me across the leather seat and whispers, 'I've been told that his ear is quite gone. The left one. Quite entirely gone.'

I turn to him so quickly that the seatbelt grabs at my neck. 'Who were you there to see?'

'Terrible thing,' Saeed spins an agate ring around the pinky finger of his hand. 'You've no doubt seen it in the papers. It's awful. A fire broke out in one of my buildings – not anything to do with the electrical system, nothing like that – and a boy was injured. A young man. Burned badly.'

'What caused the fire?'

'And he's going to be a father soon, apparently. Has a fiancée. Imagine marrying a man with no ear.'

'He'll be okay? He's going to live?'

'It isn't official yet, but the fire inspector told me what he suspects happened. He's a good man, the inspector, sharp, so I think it's safe to say that apparently this boy came home late at night drunk and fell asleep in his bed with a lit cigarette in his hand. So, nothing to do with the wiring at all.'

The car comes to a stop and I look to see where we are. The Milk Milk building, blue and white and ugly, rears up from the curb beyond my window. Saeed tells his driver to get out and open the door for me, but I say there has been a mistake.

'I don't live here anymore.'

Saeed smiles. 'Ah, mabrook! You're married now.'

I shake my head. 'I just don't live here anymore.'

Saeed apologizes and I give the driver my address. When we pull away from the Milk Milk building, I turn my head at the end of the street to make sure I do not catch sight of the sea. Even over the noise of the engine, though, I think I can hear waves.

'It's been a long time since I've seen your baba,' Saeed says, putting another piece of nicotine gum into his mouth. 'I think these things might be worse for me than the cigarettes. Too long, wallah. You're lucky to have a father like him. Sometimes I wish I hadn't been so busy when my children were young, maybe I could have stayed home more. But I do have good memories though, alhumdulillah. Remember our dinner in the desert? With the lamb and the special honeycomb from Al Hasa?'

'I remember the boy throwing fireworks into the fire.'

Saeed laughs and smacks his knee. 'Yes, yes, that was Moudi. He was a handful in those days.'

I think of telling Saeed about the days I spend with my head in the toilet, the way the water sometimes slips inside my rubber gloves carrying things that could kill me. Or maybe I will tell him that I have summoned a man made of rocks who is out on the streets tormenting people and everything is my fault. But then I see the eyes of the driver in the rearview mirror staring at me and suddenly I am too tired to speak. I clutch the soda-can lantern, pushing my fingers into the sharp borders of it, probing the place where they end and I begin.

When we pull up to my building, Saeed says goodnight, and, as the car drives off, I see Green Jack at the corner, talking to the street even though there is no one there to listen. When he finds me looking at him, he does not lift his hand to his heart and he does not bow. As I enter the front door of my apartment building, I hear his litany resume and it sounds like the beating waves of the sea have followed me home.

25 Days

I light a candle and place it into the soda-can sculpture. Putting it on the floor next to the painting of the living room and me with the wrong eyes, I'm not sure what the flame will reveal. The flicker it casts is a gentle sway of light that drifts across the gloomy painting, leavening the depths, making my eyes look something other than wrong. Making them look alive, I decide, like there is someone embedded there within the paint who is watching me from another past, from a permutation where I have remained sitting on that sofa, clenching my fingers, unchanged for all these many years.

I nudge the lantern closer to the painting, letting the light bleed across my figure. The face is not as turned away as I remember it. It seems I have found something else to look at, something besides the heavy curtains and the glare of sunlight. I look like I am trying to speak. I wonder if maybe I have an answer for my mother, a response to her confession about all the things she and my father had been seeing in me for so long. Had they seen this, I wonder, this world where I have set forth an abomination?

When I was small, I liked to sit in the kitchen and watch my mother cook, something she did while complaining about being treated like a drudge, explaining that no one ever treated her so well when she was a child.

'Do you know how lucky you are?' she would ask repeatedly.

When I tried to help, reaching up toward the stove, she would pull down a green plastic spoon from the wall and smack my arm with it. Once, when she'd finally had enough, she didn't go for the green plastic spoon, though. Instead, she took my hand and guided it toward the stove.

The pain of the hot element was a new world. I screamed and my mother cried. She clung to me, sobbing into my neck, and said that she just wanted me to understand the consequences of my actions. That she loved me enough to do that.

Sitting here, before the painting, watching the play of the flame, I think of Conestoga. I try to imagine fire spilling over my entire body. Melting my ear. I reach a finger up to its convoluted folds of cartilage and skin and wonder exactly how hot the body must get for pieces of it to melt away. That flame can swallow flesh is a thing I struggle to make sense of. I know that I must, though, because I have to understand what I have done.

And so, I bend over the soda can sculpture and its flickering flame. I move my face lower and lower toward the heat, feeling its warmth lick up the slope of my cheek, the bridge of my nose, and the soft waiting curl of my ear. This close, the glare of the candle is too much, so I squeeze my eyes shut just before I plunge into the flame.

24 Days

The pain of my ear against my pillow was so great I was never able to fall into a sleep deep enough to bring on the senseless rush of dreams, and so I wake with a brain gone hollow. When I look in the mirror, I find that my ear is red and angry – not melted away.

The missing hair at my temple is not obvious among my tangles, but the pink skin on my cheek is impossible to hide. I run a finger over it, making it crackle with hurt, thinking that I have done worse to Conestoga. Al Ghareeb is my abomination and that makes him my responsibility. When I dress, I am sure to put my knife in my pocket.

Out on the street, the souq is hectic, the crowd is shrill, and the traffic is dense and honking. At some point, without my notice, Ramadan arrived, and now as I walk down the street the restaurants and shops that were closed all day are unlocking their doors. On the street corners, men are relishing their first cigarettes after breaking their fast, exhaling huge plumes of smoke that rise like fog in the beams of the streetlamps. A grinning boy in a flawless white thobe, big blue eyes blinking, leans from a shop holding a tray of dates, offering them to everyone who passes. In every cold store, I can see stacked crates of Vimto and Tang, and cardboard cut-outs in the shape of the half-moon swaying from ceilings and rafters. There are already posters up in some windows advertising coming Eid sales, trumpeting deep discounts. I see families carrying heavy pots and covered dishes of food on their way to iftar with friends and relatives; the smell of the food clashing and mingling makes me feel lightheaded with what might be hunger or might be nausea. A little girl with thick glasses shouts hello from a balcony. Everyone on the street looks up to see who she is talking to, but she is already gone.

I find Malak coming out of a florist's shop, stumbling beneath the weight of her flowers – she has four sacks of them in her arms and is pushing a potted white bougainvillea forward with her feet. It makes a mean scraping sound on the asphalt. All around her head bob sprays of blooms, red roses and purple delphiniums and yellow sunflowers. And, at their center, she is crying.

I pick up the potted bougainvillea and Malak tells me her mother wants to see a garden again. She wants to be surrounded by flowers and plants and the smell of growing leaves and flowers dying on the vine, but because Um Malak cannot actually leave the flat any longer, Malak has to ferry plants home. This is her fifth and final trip.

'She is dying,' Malak admits as we make our way up the stairs of her apartment building.

'How much time does she have left?' I ask.

'Who knows,' Malak replies from behind the purple delphiniums. 'The doctor said it will not be long now.'

The sitting room is empty, the plastic-draped furniture dully reflecting the lamp light. But the television is on, as if we have walked into a room only recently vacated. A commercial is playing where a blonde mother and blond son spread soft cheese on crusty white bread while their voices are dubbed over in formal Arabic that makes them sound like newscasters. On the walls, there is the collection of the dead. The photograph of the unknown man in the street is hidden now, concealed behind thick folds of curtain.

I can smell Um Malak's bedroom even before we open the door, the powdery smell of too many flowers, the wet rot of soil. It makes me cough and I wonder how Um Malak is surviving it. Stepping through the door is like stepping into Al Hadiqa, every surface – the floor, the bedside tables, the bureau, the top of the cupboard, the windowsill – is fringed with flowers. Vases of white daisies frame the bed, buckets of marigolds line the foot, and, leading off into the bathroom, is a tangled trail of jasmine winding out of a plastic bag. In the corners of the room, potted palms reach the ceiling. And, in the center of it all, sitting up in bed, small eyes bright, is Um Malak.

Pushing aside a conflagration of ferns, I sit in the chair next to the bed, where my knee knocks an oxygen canister. I can now see that in the corner of the room, partially hidden by a palm leaf, there is a nurse dozing in an armchair, a magazine open on her lap.

'Life is temporary for everyone,' says Um Malak when I ask her how she is. 'Inshallah, I will have all the time I need. Anything is possible.'

Something otherworldly has befallen her voice. When she speaks, between the wheezes, her voice emerges as two voices: her usual speaking voice and a ghost voice that fluctuates both higher and lower than her own, a spectral echo.

I tell her that I agree, anything is possible. Anything, I say again, which makes her nod vigorously. When she starts coughing, I hand her a handkerchief from the stack sitting on the bedside table, but she waves me away and the cough passes.

'Will you sit with her for a minute?' Malak asks once she has set the last pot of flowers on the floor near the nurse's feet. I tell her yes, and she leaves. I know she will go sit on her balcony, flick half-smoked cigarettes into the street, and dream of the apocalypse.

Um Malak takes a breath that sounds like air moving through a wet paper bag and asks if I like her garden. 'Like Bait Azraq,' she says. 'Remember?'

I do. We used to beg her, Malak and I, to take us there to watch the puppet shows about the wise old fool Juha and his loyal donkey. The old house of Bait Azraq sat at the very edge of the souq, so close to the sea that in squally weather waves would batter the outer wall. Within the inner courtyard, around a burbling fountain, a wild garden bloomed. While Malak and I sat with the other children near the stage that was framed beneath the two lunar-white wind towers, Um Malak would stand alone against the back wall, under a hanging cloud of jasmine.

'You girls thought those puppets were real for the longest time. Malak asked me once where her strings were and who was pulling them.' Um Malak pauses between sentences to take shaking breaths. 'And I remember your favorite Juha stories. The ones with the pretty maidens and the fine horses. I also remember the one that made you cry, the one with the goat.'

'Which one?'

'The little goat that Juha killed. Puppeteers dropped the body from the rafters and it made the funniest noise. But, while everyone else was laughing, you started crying. You ran out the door onto the street, not stopping even when I shouted your name.'

There is nothing like this in my memory. Nothing at all. 'Are you sure I was there that night? I don't remember a puppet show like that.'

A noise, like wind squeezing between the cracks in a wall. She is laughing. 'You were there. You cried. You ran…' She stops and swallows heavily.

I remember Juha stories with a lost gold ring, Juha stories with a vineyard, even a Juha story of a battle, when he clanged across a battlefield waving a sword. Later, when he was asked, by an admiring puppet with blinking purple eyes, if he had had a good war, Juha's head clicked up and down. 'Yes,' he answered, 'yes, I did. I cut off the hand of my enemy.' The puppet with the purple eyes did a jig and asked Juha if after that he had cut off his enemy's head. Juha's wooden face swung left and right as he said no with his whole body. 'I didn't have to – someone else had done that before I even got there!'

But I have no memory of Juha killing a goat. No memory of the noise the body would make when dropped from the rafters. The air in Um Malak's room is so rich with flowers that when I try to take a deep breath it feels like my mouth fills with petals. Suddenly, I am desperate to leave.

'Why are you crying?' Um Malak nudges my arm with her hand.

I tell her I'm not crying, I just don't remember that night.

Her shoulders lift beneath her sheet. 'Who can remember anything anymore?'

I fight the urge to pick her up from the bed and leave this place together, as if we could outrun what is coming. I can't take my eyes off the faded purpose of her body, which is all angles and sunken places beneath her sheets. It does not seem possible that this is the same body she has lived in for so many years, that she is the same woman I knew when I was a child. I want to ask her what it feels like to be dying. If it is frightening. If it feels like falling.

There is a time of silence. Um Malak slips in and out of sleep, or a profound stillness that seems like sleep, several times. She is gone only briefly, sinking like a stone into a reservoir of calm, before resurfacing again, her eyes fluttering open, her lips mouthing strange syllables carried back from another world. The final time this happens she lifts a hand up as if to ward something off, brandishing it above her face, before letting it settle on mine. Then she watches me, her pink tongue darting out to wet her dry lips, and asks again why I am crying.

'Something is wrong,' she says. 'Is it the 'ayn? Is it still on you?'

'I don't think it was the evil eye, after all.'

'Something has happened. Something bad?'

'Something very bad.'

'Tell me,' she says, but then her eyes fall shut once again.

I watch her breathing, fast and shallow, as she once more slips away to wherever it is she keeps going.

And then I tell her. About the silver spin of Al Ghareeb's eyes, the Pyramid consumed by flame, and the goat in the desert with the serried ranks of perfect teeth. I tell her about my dreams of a broad sky, of a man in a swaybacked bed and his ear that has been burned out of existence. I tell her about my reflection, the painting, and the time that pours out of me like sweat. I tell her about the streets that are changing before our eyes, warping into different pasts and futures that might have already happened.

'It's impossible,' I say, 'it's impossible and yet I am in the very center of it. I could have killed a man, I could *still* kill a man, and I do not know what to do.'

When I finish, I stand up as quietly as possible, steadying the oxygen tank to stop it from rattling against the floor. Turning sideways so as not to disturb a water bottle serving as a vase for a thundercloud of blue orchids, I pick my way slowly around the bed. Just as I reach the armchair with the sleeping nurse, I hear movement behind me. I turn to see Um Malak sitting up, her frail arms shaking with the strain of lifting her body.

'You are a mother now,' she says. When she smiles, I see that her lips are so chapped they have dried blood at their edges.

I tell her no, I am not a mother. She has me confused with someone else. I remind her of my name and I look to the sleeping nurse, wondering if I should wake her, but Um Malak presses on.

'You said you brought someone into this world.'

I almost tell her that she is confused, that I made a mistake; I almost apologize and leave before she can say one more word. But, instead, I tell her that I have to make him leave. I have to stop something that shouldn't be possible.

'Why would you want to do that?' she asks.

'He's an abomination. He hurt someone. I don't know what he will do next.'

Um Malak's voice comes out saturated and weak, like she is speaking from beneath a mile of waves: 'When the goat dropped from the rafters do you know what you did? You ran out with your eyes closed. You couldn't see where you were going, but still you ran.'

Bait Azraq is blue and huge against its cold stretch of sky, which contains no stars and no moon, only a low haze of shredded clouds. The house is long abandoned now, and looks worn and tired. The air is damp. The sea is just around the corner and I can smell the salt. My body is tense and ready; my hand is in my pocket, fingers on the knife.

I stand for a long time trying to remember the night Um Malak told me about and, slowly, flashes return to me: the wooden figure of a small man, dressed in green, with his arms spread wide, and the sound of laughter all around. The memory is fragmented and slow, distorted in a way that feels like I am remembering a life that was not my own.

I look up at the empty windows of Bait Azraq, my eyes leaping from one to the next, expecting at any moment to find someone there watching me. The house does not feel like it is empty, and I think of Green Jack and wonder if he really is living here like I've heard – no electricity, no running water, roaming the empty rooms and treading the winding stairs, looking out on the souq from his lonely towers. I realize I have been holding my breath. In the silence I can hear the waves.

23 Days

I run the tip of my knife round and round my burnt ear. The pain is an eclipse, it is my own personal planet winking away to nothing but this. I am sitting at a table at Larvad's and people are looking. Men are looking. I am the only woman in the place. The pain makes my toes curl up in my boots. There is no telling what you could be capable of. My mother's voice has been in my head since I woke, my head full of her words, my head full of the past.

I think of a field trip to the museum when I was young. Classmates spilled out of the bus and swarmed the lobby, feet echoing against the marble floor. The teacher and the museum guide tried to calm us. They took us through the hall with the graves, the hall with the dioramas, the hall with the old tablets and chalky temple pillars. And then they took us to the pearl room, where, on the walls, lit by some subtle magic, waves rolled, and light from the far away surface fell down upon us in brilliant columns. We were on the bottom of the sea.

I push the knife harder into my ear and feel the claw of my heart heave itself up my ribcage. The pain is an immensity: I could fill the street with it. The street. Outside of Larvad's, people are in coats, scarves, hats. The real cold has come. A white cat sits on the sidewalk, not moving when people step over it or almost on it. The cat just looks at the door of Larvad's wondering about food. Inside, at the table across from me, two men are watching me while they eat. Yellow rice clings to their fingers. They could be father and son.

Cases of pearls glowed in the shifting light in the room at the museum. All colors; soft pink, purple black, milky cream, purest white. For thousands of years, the guide said, pearls were what the Gulf was known for. We have very special water here, she continued, a mixture of salt water from the sea and fresh water from undersea springs. 'Barzakh,' she said, 'Barzakh. The whole of the Gulf is a barzakh.' I thought of the grave, but I knew that wasn't the meaning she was after. And, she continued, it is believed that this special mix of water is why our pearls are considered the best in the world. From a cabinet, she removed a small bowl containing three seed pearls and passed it among us. When I held one of the tiny pearls up to the light, there was a sheen on its surface that was almost a reflection. But not quite. No matter how closely I looked, I could never bring about a resolution.

I push harder into my ear with the knife, waiting for my body to fold itself around the epicenter of the pain. The pressure is tremendous. The father and son with yellow rice clinging to their fingers are now working their way through a dosa. The father says something to his son, lifts his chin at me, and the son stares at the knife in my hand. I think of Conestoga's missing ear and wonder if he will vanish along with it.

The pearls went back into the cabinet. 'Next,' the museum guide said, 'we will learn about how these pearls were brought up from the bottom of the sea.' She guided us to a corner of the large room where we discover a man hanging from the ceiling. As we got closer, I saw it was not a man but a fake man, a mannequin with green eyes and a clip on his nose. Around his waist there was a small pouch and a knife. When I got right up next to him, I saw that the brown paint on his feet was flaking away, revealing the bone-white material beneath. The boy standing beside me asked the guide if the man was dead.

I work the knife faster now, scraping a track in the crevices of my ear, no longer careful with the edge of the blade, as I remember the words of the witness on the street as we all stood there watching the smoke pour up toward the moon. Conestoga in his bed and the unnatural flames moving too fast. I dreamed a thing and then it happened. The father and son finish their dosa. They drink their glasses of lassi. They go to the counter to pay, and I see them say something to the cashier. The cashier calls for Larvad, and their heads all bend forward, coming together. After a moment, Larvad looks out of the kitchen. He says something to the father and son and opens the door for them to leave. A gust of cold wind, a trilling meow. The cat leaps into the open doorway, a splash of white leaving the dark street. Larvad kicks it back out.

'The divers' eardrums would sometimes rupture,' the guide said, lifting a hand to the side of her face and splaying her fingers out with a jarring quickness. The boy beside me lifted his own hands to his face and cringed. 'At the bottom of the sea,' the guide continued, 'there were sharks and snakes and poisonous jellyfish, but it was said that it was the great pressure that the divers feared most. Because they had to go down to the bottom and back up to the surface again and again, their bodies were never able to reach an equilibrium, they were in a constant state of disorienting flux. They believed this could drive a person mad.'

'You cannot do this here,' Larvad is saying to me. He started off saying it quietly, but when I didn't move he got louder. His knuckles rest on my table. 'Go somewhere else, you are troubling my customers. Why are you like this?' His face has gone red and his nose is dripping.

I tell him that things are going wrong, that I am under tremendous pressure.

'You leave right now,' he says, reaching out for my sleeve and yanking me to my feet.

When I stumble out the door, I see the white cat dash into the street. She slinks under a parked car, her delicate tail swishing. At the end of the road, a car honks and she hurtles forward, just missing the wheels of a delivery van. Now, she is in the middle of the street and cars split around her, honking. I watch as the driver of a black sedan spots her. The car surges forward, swerving into the next lane to line up with her perfectly. The white cat turns her head, sees what is about to hit her, and leaps.

22 Days

The sound of a key in my lock. I am instantly awake. I scramble out of my bed and grab the knife from under my pillow.

Into the bathroom. Lock the door and back up against the far wall. The sound of footsteps. My fingers around the knife are shaking and slick with sweat.

I look up at the small vent over the toilet, wondering if I could cram myself through there. But, even if I could, we are five stories off the ground. There would be nowhere to go.

I hear a voice. I tell myself that when the time comes I will be ready to fight. He will come through the bathroom door and I will swing my arm and the blade will flash through the light and find his body. But then I am thinking about dying here in this soggy bathroom, with the mold near the ceiling and the always damp towels on the floor, and I feel the sting of bile rising up my throat.

The person moving through my flat clicks on the light, from beneath the bathroom door there comes a flood of yellow.

'Hello?'

I was expecting the sound of hooves.

'Hello, dear, are you home?'

Breath snakes out of me. My body feels leaden and sick, but also too light, as if pieces of me are floating up while other pieces are crumpling to the ground. I unlock the bathroom door and push it open. Mrs Al Jabri is standing by my bed, looking around my flat.

Seeing me, she frowns. 'You can't leave this food out, dear! This is not clean. You want my building to have rats? Rodents bring disease, you know. You can't live here if—'

'You can't just barge in here,' I say.

Mrs Al Jabri tuts. 'My building, my rules.'

Another figure steps forward. Clipped black hair, tidy mustache, eyes that point in different directions.

'Good evening,' Officer Bayan says. 'Why don't you put that knife down?'

I clench it more firmly.

'And look at these sheets! I've never seen sheets this dirty in my life.'

'I need you to put that down. I'm just here to ask you a few questions.'

'I have nothing to say. I don't want you here.'

'Dear, what is this? Did you start a *fire* here? It looks like something has been burned. Who lives like this?'

Officer Bayan takes another step toward me. He is now so close to the bathroom door that I couldn't slip by and run out of the flat even if I wanted to. He is not a big man, but he is tall and his arms are long. I would be caught. He watches me place the knife on the rim of the sink.

I sit on my bed and watch Mrs Al Jabri open my refrigerator. When she sees that it isn't working, that it is black and hot inside, she reminds me that I'm killing her. Officer Bayan asks her to leave, and though she looks pained by the request, she does. He closes the front door behind her and asks me how I am.

'Fine.'

'Good. That's good.' He looks around the flat. There is dirty underwear by the kitchen and across the small table are a dozen wadded up tissues from my last bloody nose. In a semi-circle around the bed are the dirty dishes and tea cups Mrs Al Jabri had been so upset by. By the painting there are a dozen candles and a spill of blackened matches. 'I suppose after what happened you still aren't feeling your best. It's not every day you get run over by a car.'

I know he is only saying this to save me from embarrassment, so that we can both pretend my apartment is crawling in cockroaches and grime because of the accident, and I hate him for it. I hate his conscientious pity and the way he stands in the center of my flat like he has a right to be here and the way one of his nervous eyes keeps sliding over to me when he smiles. I think about my knife and how much better it would be if it were still in my hand.

'We heard you checked yourself out against medical advice,' Bayan continues. 'Why would you do that?'

'I don't like hospitals.'

He laughs. 'Neither do I. Awful places. I hear doctors kill more people accidentally than cancer and heart attacks combined. Do you think that's true? I read it in an airplane magazine, but I don't know. I hope not.'

He crosses to the window and moves aside the curtain to look down on the street. Color from neon lights flickers over his face, red and green and then blue. He frowns as if he has seen something out there that he doesn't like and he pulls the curtain shut again.

'When we last spoke, if you remember, I mentioned someone had gotten in touch with us.'

I nod.

'Well, she, ah, she seemed to be of the opinion that you… that you might have possibly,' his voice stumbles, 'well, she thought maybe you had thrown yourself in front of the car.'

She? The person who contacted Officer Bayan was a *woman*? This had not occurred to me. I shift on the bed and my foot disturbs a tea mug. It hits the floor with a dull thud and from inside a stream of brown liquid trickles out.

'Do you have any paper towels? I could get that for you,' Officer Bayan says, gesturing toward the kitchen.

'I thought you said there weren't any witnesses. When you came to see me the day after the accident, you said you had asked at all the shops along the street and in the apartments upstairs. No one saw anything. That's what you said.'

'You remember that? You were so out of it that I didn't think you would remember anything.' Using a dirty towel from the bathroom he mops up the spill. Kneeling this close to me I can smell him – cologne, something like wood and leather. Clutching the towel his hands are small and refined, his fingernails chewed down raw. I watch him work the floor clean.

He tilts his head toward the bathroom. 'You have a lot of knives?'

'Am I in trouble?'

'Not at all.' He sucks air through his teeth as he stands up, as if it hurts him to rise. 'We're just concerned.'

'About me?'

'About you.'

'Why?'

'Well, if you, ah, if you did possibly throw yourself into traffic, then that would be concerning. Don't you agree?'

'I already told you what happened. Why would you believe a witness when I already told you?'

'It's not about believing or not believing, it's about being thorough. We just want to explore all possible permutations of the story.'

Permutations. She. I think of the putty-pink envelope hiding beneath my bed and the look on the archeologist's face as he carried the old painting through the cemetery.

'Who was the witness?'

He rubs a finger down the bridge of his nose, and I wait for him to tell me that that isn't important, that he isn't going to tell me who it was, but instead, he asks me when was the last time that I spoke to my mother.

'My mother? My mother told you that she saw me step in front of traffic?'

'Ah, no. Not exactly.' Officer Bayan looks again to the bathroom. 'But she did tell us that you are a danger to yourself. And possibly to others.'

I run my hand across the dirty sheets of my bed and they feel oily; I can't remember the last time they were washed. In the corners above the window there are cobwebs, but there are no spiders. The light coming in from beneath the front door flickers – I know that on the other side Mrs Al Jabri has her ear pressed firmly to the door.

'You called her a witness, but she's not.'

'Well, no. Not strictly speaking. But wouldn't you agree she has some insight into how you might be feeling? She is worried about you. You know how mothers are.'

When I don't answer, he pulls a card from his jacket pocket and puts it on the table, tapping it with his fingers.

'You'll call if you need us?'

I stay quiet and he seems to take that as an answer. As he reaches the door, he tells me goodnight and tells me to take good care of myself.

I stand up. I feel the sticky spill of tea against my left foot. Looking Officer Bayan in the eye, I tell him that I am capable of anything. 'Anything,' I say, repeating the word, letting it hang there between us.

'Yes,' he says, backing away from me. 'Of course you are.'

21 Days

'I hear that you have been having some difficulty and that you'll be withdrawing from the university,' Dr Garza said.

This was after I had walked myself sick on my college campus, stumbling through rain and hail until I found myself at the very center of something I did not understand, hoof prints stamped on the ground at my feet. Dr Garza's office in the campus medical center was blue, a dozen shades of it, and it had an aquarium that held three yellow fish. While she introduced herself to me, ran over her qualifications, what I could expect from speaking to her, made me sign the necessary forms, I watched the fish wheel and dive through their small glass world. Things that live in water seem too flimsy for survival and these fish were no different – their fins were translucent and, in places, looked to be dissolving. Specks of tissue drifted through the water, and I wondered if it needed to be cleaned. When the fish breathed through their gills, did they suck in these particles that used to be their body? Did they know they were living on themselves? When I began to feel sick, I looked away.

Dr Garza told me to call her Patricia. Or Patty, if I was so inclined. She looked young, but the date on the medical degree on the wall told me she wasn't.

There was a pen and notepad on her lap. 'Do you want to tell me about your difficulties?'

I crossed my legs at the ankles and avoided looking at my feet.

She jotted something down and I saw that her pen had purple ink. This made me angry. The childish stupidity of a grown woman writing in purple ink, in an office that stunk like a fish store. But then the anger was gone – as quickly as it had come, it left me.

She asked me about going 'back over there'. Was I looking forward to that? Why didn't I tell her about it.

So, I did. I told her about the souq and the people of the souq and the mother and father I had and the things they had said and done and the small body of the dead goat and the sound of the waves and the sharp click of a lock on my bedroom door and the nosebleeds and the air-raid sirens and the gas masks and the electrons with all their terrible distance and time, above all, I told her about time and the secret truths it was hiding.

When I finished speaking, Dr Garza had filled three pages of her notebook. This made me think of her three fish, each one bouncing its face against the glass of the tank, wondering what monstrous figures it was seeing. Then Dr Garza spoke to me for some time – about the things I had told her, what it meant, and what it had done. When our time was up, she asked if she could hug me, and then she wished me well.

My first week back home, I stayed in bed and floated in a waterlogged world, my brain reverberating with the things Dr Garza had said. It wasn't until my mother told me she was leaving that I spoke.

We were in my bedroom. Moving around my room, running her finger over my books, my jewelry box, the small figurines I kept on my bureau, my mother looked beautiful. She was giddy. Excitement rippled off her body, venting from her pores. She was telling me about a man, the man she was leaving my father to be with. She told me she had known him since high school, when they were both at boarding school in Beirut, back when she still felt like herself. Back before she somehow got lost on the way. He was a kind man, a good man, she told me.

'When he wrote to let me know he was coming here and that he wanted to see me, I couldn't say no. I just couldn't. I've been unhappy for so long and I know you've been unhappy seeing me like that. By doing this, I'm making us both happy. You see?' Her voice was little girl eager, her wide eyes startled by this apparent good luck. She was too radiant, a thing I could not look at directly.

'The past isn't gone,' I said, not knowing any other way to begin. And then I told her about my appointment with Dr Garza, what I had spoken to her about and what she had said in return. The way terrible things had a way of living on and on in time.

As my mother listened, she stopped moving and stood still at the center of my room. I remembered the fish in Dr Garza's aquarium, the way they were coming undone all along the edges. Watching my mother, I could see that she was doing the same.

When I finished, spotlights of color flamed in her cheeks.

'How dare you?' she asked. For a moment I thought she might cry. 'How *dare* you? How could you tell a stranger all those lies about how we treated you? Believe me when I say I've never known a more spoiled child. You have everything I wanted when I was your age.' I thought she was going to say something else, there was something hanging right there in her mind for her to say, I could see it. She stood there staring down at me for so long that I imagined we would never leave that room, that we would always be disintegrating together in that moment of time. But she never said another word to me.

Three days later, she left with two suitcases full of clothes and a hat box full of her paints. I watched from the living-room window as a man with a grey beard helped her load her things into his small white car. He had a long, loping grace as he moved from the curb into the street, his hand resting on her lower back. She kept laughing, as if everything he said was funny. She was pretending to be a different kind of person, weighed down by nothing. I waited for her to look up at me, to wave goodbye, but she didn't. When they drove away, I imagined I could still hear her laughing.

My father stayed in his study all that day. I had never heard him argue with my mother or try to stop what was happening. When it was time for dinner that night, he came to my bedroom and opened the door.

'Good evening,' he said, pulling something out of his pocket. In the murky evening light, I could see it was a small handful of cash. He sat it on my bureau where the edges of the bills twitched in the current of air from the ceiling fan. He watched them for a moment, making sure they wouldn't scatter to the floor. When he cleared his throat, the skin at the back of my neck began to tingle.

'You can't live here if you aren't in school,' he said. 'And as you aren't in school, you need to move out. You have one week.'

He then turned and walked down the hallway toward the kitchen. He was in his stockinged feet, and the sound of his footsteps on the carpet was gentle. As I listened to him opening and closing cabinet doors as he prepared his supper, I realized those were the first words he had spoken to me since I had left for America.

20 Days

I don't remember leaving my flat. There is a fine mist in the night air and I think I have been walking for a long time. I breathe deeply the wetness and try to recall which direction I came from, but there is nothing. Just the knowledge that I am walking and have been walking for some time. There is an ache in my feet and a pain at the base of my skull. I think maybe it has been there for weeks. Longer, maybe. Maybe always.

I come across a mural that is done; the first I've seen that is finished. A hundred fish swarm through a towering wave that crashes from one side of the building to the other. The water is turbulent and grey, choked with silt.

I stand for a few minutes or hours looking at them, letting their colors course through my eyes until I can see them swimming in my vision even when I blink. I slide up to them and run my fingers across their rippling flanks and thick fins, telling myself that they aren't real, that I am not wading across the sea floor filling my lungs with salt water. When I finally leave the alley behind, I wait to see if the fish will follow, so realistic do they look that I can imagine them breaching off the wall to fling their flimsy bodies across the road.

At the end of the block, I pass a wall covered in graffiti, with squiggles of names in Arabic, English, Tagalog, and Urdu, and a single flower, a daisy, drawn treacherously large. Behind this wall is the old London Club. It's gone to ruin now, but years ago there were tennis courts, stables, a pub, a restaurant. One summer, an old man had a heart attack while swimming in the pool and died right there in the water. Liam was there at the time, said it took four lifeguards to heave the body out of the deep end. For weeks afterward, the whole street reeked of chlorine as the pool attendants worked to reassure everyone that the remnants of shit and urine voided from his bobbing body were completely gone. We told ghost stories about the dead man for the rest of that year, each of us claiming we had seen his waterlogged body leaking in these alleys.

By the time I reach the hospital I have myself convinced that this time I will go inside. I will find Conestoga and into his remaining ear I will pour out my story. Apologize. Explain how things are, how things were, how too many streets led me to this. Then I think of his hand on my wrist, the pain at the top of the stairs, and think maybe he will do the same.

I stop and lean back, looking up the pale exterior of the building, pockmarked with black windows, and I remember that I stayed here once. I had just started high school and I vomited whenever I ate anything. Not because I wanted to. My body did it without me, curving violently around whatever it was I put into my belly. When I fainted in school from dehydration, my mother demanded the doctors fix me. She brought me to this hospital and they gave me a room that looked out onto this street, where nothing ever happened.

One night in the hospital my father came to see me. My mother had gone home to shower and change her clothes and she had insisted he come keep me company. I was surprised that he did. When he entered the room, he coughed, but it wasn't a real cough. It was just something to do to fill the silence. He stood by the window, staring down at the street. The skin around his nose and mouth was tight, as if he was trying not to breathe in too deeply. For a long time, we didn't speak. We listened to distant car horns and the sound of the nurses walking along the corridor just outside.

'Your mother says you kept your breakfast down,' he broke the silence gently. His voice was little more than a murmur.

'It's the medicine they gave me,' I said. I was unsure if I should sit up or stay lying down, so I settled for propping myself up on an elbow.

'They figure it out yet?'

'The doctor said it could be just nerves.'

My father snorted. 'What do you have to be nervous about?'

'That's just what he said.'

'Well, you've got your mother in a right state. I don't think she's slept all week.'

'I'm sorry.'

He then said he guessed he needed to be getting back home, but he didn't leave.

He just stayed standing there, looking out at the street below. I had never seen him in a hospital before and he looked out of place, like a book that had been put back on the shelf backwards. Behind his back, his left hand was in constant motion – it clenched and unclenched, not stopping.

I'd first noticed that particular tic earlier that year, after a phone call woke me up in the dead of night. Leaving my bedroom, moving through the long, dark hallway of our flat, I heard a muffled voice. Still hazy with sleep, to me it sounded like it wasn't even speaking a proper language, just making hushed, disembodied noises at random.

Peering into the kitchen, which was lit only by the orange light coming from the oven hood, I saw my father in his robe leaning against the counter, the phone pressed against his ear. His voice was still quiet, but now I could hear him saying 'no'. He said it many times. Behind his back, I watched his hand clenching and unclenching, faster and faster. It looked like a racing heart.

I learned later that the phone call had come from my grandfather. My father's mother was ill and she wanted to see her son, but my father refused to go. When we got another late-night phone call, a few weeks later, once again I found my father standing in the kitchen holding the phone to his ear. This time, though, he wasn't saying 'no.' He wasn't saying much of anything. He listened, taking in whatever message was being delivered, and then he cleared his throat, hard, and hung up the phone. When he walked out of the room, he told me that his mother was dead.

'You know,' my father said, after standing silently for a long time at my hospital room window, 'I was much younger than you when I learned something very important.'

'What?'

He turned to face me for the first time. 'If you want to get up out of that bed and stop being sick, you can. It's all up to you.'

There was suddenly too much saliva in my mouth. I swallowed and it caught at the back of my throat. 'It doesn't feel like that to me,' I said.

'It doesn't matter what it *feels* like. I learned, when I was still just a boy, that all that matters is what we can control. And,' he continued, 'all we can control is ourselves. That is all there is in the world.'

He turned back to the window.

'Have you looked out here yet?' he asked.

'I don't think there's anything much to see.'

'There's always something to see,' he said, 'if you want to see it.'

=

Still leaning back, I find the window of my old hospital room, and remember the view of nothing that it gave me. I wonder which window belongs to Conestoga, and what he can see from within. This late, most of the windows are concealed behind curtains. But some reveal light. There is one in particular that keeps drawing my eye. On the fourth floor. Its light is faint, not like hospital light at all, and one of the curtains is closed, while the other is open. It is a half-shut eye slantways peering at the street. He could be in there even now, behind the glass, without his ear, watching me.

19 Days

The villa is a honeycomb of in-between spaces and open-air hallways that lead onto palm-shrouded atriums and gloomy courtyards – all of them full of people. Bars and nightclubs are shut for the duration of Ramadan, so parties like this are even more crowded than usual. From somewhere I can hear live music, someone with an oud and a timorous voice. A waiter passes me carrying a tray of empty glasses. When he smiles, I see a flash of metal inside his mouth, a tongue ring. Near a fountain, a woman with a stark black bob is discussing the mural project with a group of listeners.

'Chaos,' she says, 'it's causing chaos everywhere. The painters are running amok, getting in the way of traffic, going rogue, painting on any wall they want – even ones they aren't meant to touch.'

Another woman, holding a glass of wine, asks her when the artist will return. 'He needs to take his crew in hand,' she says, gesturing with her wineglass, leaking a slop of red onto the ground.

The woman with the bob answers that there is no way to tell, he comes and goes as he likes. 'We are at his mercy,' she concludes.

Liam and Abdullah left me to find the bar when we first arrived and I have not seen them since. I asked Liam whose villa this was and he said he didn't know. Abdullah said he thought it might actually belong to one of his cousins, but Liam told him it didn't count when everyone was your cousin. Then he told me not to ask questions like that because it gave away the fact that I didn't belong.

Leaving the courtyard, I follow the music up a flight of stairs – geometric carvings in the outer wall let in a cold wind. When I met Liam and Abdullah on the street by the karak stand, Liam insisted I come with them. He pushed me down the sidewalk, telling me that it was Sinjin's leaving do and that I had to say goodbye. But now that I am here, I haven't seen Sinjin or anyone that he knows. It is a strange crowd. Braying faces and expensive coats. Women in heels that raise them off the ground by several inches and men with heavy watches made of gold. On the landing of the stairs, I pass a couple in a heated conversation, their heads bowed toward each other. The woman catches my eye and smirks.

At the top of the stairs, I find a long colonnaded room that ends in a wide balcony. Leaning over the railing I see yet another courtyard below, one that has mosaic tiles on the floor and flowering borders along the walls. I am watching the odd shapes cast along the ground by the swaying vines of honeysuckle when two figures appear at either side of me.

'Well, he's not going to make it,' Liam says, leaning his elbows on the railing. 'We saw Lubna and she says her brother knows a nurse at the hospital where Caleb is, and he might not make it. The burns are apparently severe.'

Abdullah, from my other side, tells Liam to stop saying that. 'That's not exactly what she said, stop being dramatic. He's probably going to pull through.'

'It's weird,' Liam continues. 'We were at Shamrock together like a month ago. A month! And now he's going to die? Too fucking weird. You know he's going to be a father?'

I say yes.

'*Was* going to be a father,' Liam says.

'Stop it,' Abdullah says.

'Although,' Liam says, 'I could never really believe that he let himself get tied down.'

'Not like it slows him down much,' Abdullah says.

'True. I lost track of how many of our nights out ended with him getting clocked by some guy saying he was hitting on his girlfriend.'

'At least he knew how to take a punch,' Abdullah says.

Remembering the hospital windows last night, I ask if they have gone to visit him.

'We tried,' Liam says. 'But I think only Fernanda can get in to see him. Being his wife and all.'

'Fiancée,' Abdullah corrects.

Liam shrugs. 'Same difference.'

In the courtyard below, there is a man in a thobe with a hooded falcon on his arm. A photographer follows and people gather in small groups to have their photo taken with the tawny bird. Its talons are curved and gleaming. I watch as it lifts its smooth head, hearing something in the distance.

Liam turns to face me. 'Before the fire Caleb had a lot to say about you.'

'Oh?'

'Oh yes.'

'What?'

'He said you were a tease.' Liam's smile is sharp and mocking. 'That you say one thing and do another.'

'Does he say anything about what *he* does?'

'He said that when you two were at Copper Top things were just starting to get somewhere when you tried to push him down the stairs. And you tried to tell us you didn't even know him.'

'I didn't know his name was Caleb.'

'You didn't even know his name?' Liam laughs, shaking his head.

The deeper we go into the house searching for Sinjin, the stranger the party becomes. There is more music pouring from more rooms, all of it discordant, as if a dozen different parties have been forced to share the same space. I see the woman who earlier spilled her wine now in a corner crying. She is using the hem of her pale-green scarf to dab at her eyes, as she watches a couple dance to music that is going too slow for the beat they are keeping.

In one room there are two belly dancers snaking their hips in lazy circles, their sheer pants revealing dimpled thighs. Men clutching glasses of champagne stalk the perimeter of this room, as if they are building up their courage for something. In another room, we find half a dozen tall hookahs burbling and people lounging on velvet cushions exhaling plumes of smoke that churn across the high ceiling.

Taking in the scene, Liam rolls his eyes and says, loudly, that the whole party is like a bad joke. A wiry man, who is using a pair of tongs to place a glowing coal onto a hookah, hears this and looks up. Abdullah puts a hand on Liam's shoulder and maneuvers him quickly out of the room.

Working our way through a long atrium that has a row of dried olive trees planted in the center of the floor, I listen to Abdullah telling Liam that he wants to leave. I can tell that he's trying to be patient, his voice low and soothing, but Liam stalks off, saying he needs another drink. Abdullah follows him into the crowd.

Left alone, I hear a voice I recognize. I turn and see the tour guide who is also a shopkeeper. He is polished tonight, his hair slicked back and glossy, his suit jacket a gunmetal grey. I nod at him, but if he recognizes me he doesn't betray it, he just keeps up his stream of conversation with the three women gathered around him.

'It was all a hoax. All of it.'

'But why? Why would anyone do that?' The woman asking the question emphasizes her curiosity by placing a hand on the tour guide's elbow. There is a ring on every finger and, when she presses her body into him, her silk dress strains across her hips.

'The real question is *how*,' the tour guide says. 'He fooled more than a few people – some of whom should have known better.'

'What will they do now?'

'They've told the archeologist he has to clear out. They're bringing in a team from Egypt to clean up his mess and figure out what exactly it was that he found. There *was* something there, in actuality, something of interest, in the tablet. He just tried to make it out to be something that it wasn't. Like I said all along, there never was any new god.'

'How very odd,' the woman in the silk dress says, swaying once more into the tour guide's side. He looks down at her and smiles.

When I find Sinjin he is at the center of a group of people standing near an open window. The window has no glass, and cold air shuttles through, smelling of car exhaust and fried food. There are so many different conversations battling around us, in so many different languages, that, at first, I don't understand what Sinjin is saying to me. He reaches out and grabs my arm, pulling me toward him.

'I said, you'll be next.'

Against my burned ear his lips feel like moving paper, crackly and dry.

'What do you mean?' I try to pull myself away, but he holds me close.

'The next one who has to leave. It'll be you.'

'Why would you say that?'

'You think you have anything to offer? More than me? Why should you stay if I can't? Omar won't need you to file papers and water plants forever. You'll be next.'

He then drops my arm and reels backward. I realize he's drunk. He has new glasses now, ones made of thin wire that look painful against the bridge of his nose.

'I am leaving,' he says, each word lobbed at me like a stone. I tell him I know. 'I have to go back *home*,' he continues, then lifts his hands into the air and does air quotes, even though he has stopped speaking and there is nothing to put quotes around.

'I'm sorry.'

From another room I can hear the sound of someone barking like a dog. Or maybe it is a real dog, trapped in these many parties. The noise is becoming a howl, a raw desperate cry, and then there is the sound of shattering glass and the barking stops.

'Being born foreign. It makes you stand like this,' Sinjin goes on, spreading his legs wide, like he is going to drop into the splits.

From the other side of the room Liam spots him and whistles.

'One foot in this world. No, two feet in other worlds. Wait.' Using my shoulder for balance, Sinjin rights himself and tries again. 'Each foot in a different world. That's it. So now I go home. And someday all of this, all of you, will be just a time that I remember. You won't be anything but that.'

He pushes me away, falling into the crowd, and I wish that I had never come to the party. I've seen too many scenes like this over the years – crowded houses full of melodramatic tableaus, tears and promises to never forget, all of it tinged with a manic sincerity that makes my head hurt. Living here, living like this, means people pass through your life like comets punching through the sky on their way elsewhere. Malak told me once that her mother warned her never to make friends with an expat because all we do is come and go.

I watch Sinjin reach Liam, who claps him around the shoulders and insists he have another drink. He tries to keep moving out of the room, but Liam holds him back by both arms, laughing and shouting things I cannot quite hear.

Liam had said that Conestoga was going to die, but Abdullah had said that he was probably going to live. I wonder whose version of the story lives closest to the truth. I think back to the moment in the Copper Top hallway, when Conestoga was pulling my arm up over my head, when his mouth was on mine, and I think how strange it is that I was kissing a man who now exists somewhere between living and dying.

I stand here for a long time, watching Liam force a drink into Sinjin's hands, watching the tour guide charm the laughing women, watching this room full of people who likewise exist somewhere between living and dying. I tell myself that someday all of this will be just a time I remember, and it won't mean anything but that.

18 Days

His ear is gone and there is blood on my face. Tubes, clear and fat, drip fluid into his veins. A white bandage wound around his skull is speckled with blood and there is blood on my face. Someone is gasping and I think it is Conestoga, but he is asleep. Not asleep, unconscious. The whole of this ward reeks and there are mechanical beeps coming from machines everywhere. The clockwork march of his body is being reordered. Someone is gasping and I realize it is me. Now my sleeve is soaked with blood so I switch, lifting my left arm up to my face to stem the tide pouring from my nose. A nurse will come soon. I will be found soon. I snuck past them and no one saw me, but I left a trail of bloody droplets searching for his ward and I am certain there will come a moment when I am discovered.

I tell myself that Conestoga does not look like someone who is about to die. There is only the one bandage on the left side of his head, just covering his ear, and it isn't even that big. His face looks like it looked when I first met him, tanned and wide, with thick skin and a long nose. Despite the rhythmic beeps and the strange smells, this isn't the intensive care unit. And his breathing is steady, gentle even. Maybe what Liam said was only a rumor. Maybe Liam doesn't even know what he's talking about at all. An embryonic feeling of relief, that everything might still somehow turn out alright, trickles up from my belly, and it is so powerful I have to reach out and steady myself on the foot of the bed.

Conestoga's lips part slowly and the moan that emerges is thick and coarse. Within it there is not just pain, but fear. Even in this heavy, drugged sleep, there is fear. I yank my hand off the bed and step away. He shifts slightly and the sheet slips down his chest, revealing the rest of what I have done.

There is another bandage running the width of his torso, another wraps his forearm, and, beneath the sheets,

I realize that one of his legs is thicker than the other, made bigger than it should be by what must be another layer of bandages. The burns go from his face all down the length of his left side. His eyelids flutter, and his moan gets louder, higher, wind whistling through a narrow pass, and I splutter on something, my mouth filling with the taste of time and salt. Another hot gush from my nose, blood on the floor. I clap a hand over my face and run.

17 Days

I wake to the memory of flame on flesh, flesh on flame – fingers moving through it, caressing it, dancing with it – but it is not until I sit up and look at the painting leaning against the wall at the foot of my bed that the memory returns in its entirety. It is the sofa that does it, the sad green of it, somber in the too-bright light, the angle it makes against the carpet. I remember what it felt like to take sanctuary behind its bulky mass, to run my finger across the rough fabric and eavesdrop on conversations that I didn't entirely understand. And others that I did.

The night of the flesh-on-flame, my mother was hosting a dinner party. This was after the war and, with so many people returning to the city, my mother was eager to entertain. She had a habit of collecting people. Sweeping them into her orbit. She would bring her new friends to our flat and try to impress them with her best imitation of how they themselves might behave at their own home. Her voice would change slightly, her accent modulating itself when necessary, and she would use different words and hold new opinions. There were nights when we ate enchiladas, nights when we ate biriyani, and nights when we listened to Tchaikovsky and dipped pieces of dark bread into pots of molten cheese. Our guests were like the furniture my mother so frequently changed, moving in and out of our rooms, leaving behind only the faintest traces of themselves.

But on the night of flesh-on-flame, I was too unwell to meet the guests, having suffered an asthma attack bad enough to keep me home from school for two days. I was told to stay in bed and I did, until I heard the guests arrive. Then, I sat at my open bedroom door and listened as they had drinks in the living room. I heard the pop of a champagne bottle, which told me something about this couple and who my mother was trying to be tonight.

When my mother summoned everyone to the dining room, I watched them troop across the end of the hall. I remember the male guest clearly: a man, older than my parents, with grey hair and stooped shoulders, wearing a tweed jacket with elbow patches.

When they had all passed into the dining room, I snuck down the hall and slipped into my place behind the sofa. From here, I could not be seen unless someone leaned over the back of it, which no one had ever done. It was an ideal spot for spying because I could hear most of the conversations from the dining room and then, once they moved back to the living room for after dinner drinks, I could hear it all. Better still, if I was careful, I could lean slightly to one side and, through the legs of the side table, catch sight of whichever guest happened to sit in one of the chairs by the window.

There was the clink and jangle of cutlery. The smell of roast beef and horseradish sauce. A laugh spilled out of the dining room. My mother. No matter who she was entertaining, no matter who she had become, there was always that laugh, the tumbling fall of it exactly the same. Behind the sofa, my inhales began to feel tight and scratchy – the portent of another asthma attack. It felt like spiders darting across my lungs.

'It's like they are born knowing what buttons to press,' the female guest, a sleek older woman, said. 'Like they have a manual or something.'

'Exactly! That is exactly right!' My mother and her laugh.

'And it's such a gamble. You never know how your child will turn out, if they will be anything like you or not. For us, they were always such surprises. Such maddening surprises!'

'Oh, I think our daughter is quite like me,' my mother said. 'She likes all the things I like and she seems to think the same way. I like to think of her as my best friend.'

'But I'm sure when she throws a tantrum it still gets under your skin!'

'Oh, yes!' My mother's laugh grew sharp enough to cut.

Then came a ponderous voice that could only be the older man, thick and clotted.

'Tantrums are not tantrums,' he said, 'but cries for help. Children do not have the skills of an adult, they need us to bolster them. That's a parent's job.'

'Bolster,' my mother responded, her voice contemplative. 'Now, that is an interesting way to put it. Bolster. I have to confess, sometimes I think it feels more like smother.'

'To the adult or the child?' the older woman replied.

Laughter. The voices melted together.

As I knew they would, the women gathered the dishes off the table and moved into the kitchen. I heard running water and tinfoil being spread over serving dishes. Into the living room came the men. I heard a match being struck and smelled the scent of a pipe. The spiders in my lungs began to scramble.

'Delicious meal. Your wife is quite a cook. Thank you for having us.'

Peeking out I saw the older man in the tweed jacket settle himself in the wingback chair by the window. He reached out and examined the antique snuffbox on the side table. In the lamplight, I noticed a purple mark on his forehead, a zebiba, from prayer.

My father took the chair next to him and lit his own pipe. He then used the match to light a stubby green candle. The scent of pine bloomed. There were a few minutes of silence as the men smoked and the women cleaned.

Then my father asked the old man if he might ask him a question.

'Certainly,' the man replied.

Crouched on the floor, my knee pressed into the back of the green sofa, my spiders turned in unison to listen to what was to come. I could not resist peeking out from behind the couch once more to take in the scene and, just as I did, I saw my father's eyes, blank and flat, slide in my direction. I fell back instantly, but I knew it was too late; I had been seen. I waited to be hauled to my bedroom. But nothing happened, no one came.

'I'd like to ask you something about your field,' my father said. I could hear a mouthful of smoke in the way he formed his words.

'Of course.'

'You must see a range of attitudes among parents. In how they feel about their children. Some good, some bad.'

'That is to be expected. Parenting is never easy.'

'Really? I haven't found it particularly challenging. Not in the way you mean, I don't think.'

'No?'

'No, but I do have to laugh at the dishonesty of it.'

'Dishonesty?'

'Well, the dishonesty around it, I suppose I should say. The way it seems like all of society colludes into funneling us down this path.'

'I'm not sure I follow.'

'Well, I used to think of marriage and children as the thing one does. It was just a part of life that simply couldn't be avoided. It wasn't until I already found myself within it, with a wife and a child, that I realized there were other paths that I could have taken. The whole institution of it, marriage and children, it stifles the mind, doesn't it?'

'I suppose for some people, yes, it could feel like that.'

'Precisely. A stifling. And the oddest thing is the lies that come with it, wouldn't you say?'

'The lies?'

'That it all brings happiness.'

'Ah.'

'The whole charade of it. That one can enjoy any of it.'

'You don't?'

'I don't think many people do, if I'm honest. I know my parents didn't. Motherhood drove my mother mad. I mean that quite literally. It snuffs the life out of you. It all seems, I don't know, it all seems so very small.'

'I see. You wanted to ask me something?'

'Well, not ask, necessarily – run by you, I suppose. You being the expert in the field, family psychologist and all. I'm sure to you all of this is very normal, very boring stuff, conversations like this. But for those of us stuck in the middle of it, well. It's just that, it's just that I wonder sometimes: is it normal for a father to not *like* his child?'

The older man coughed.

'I mean, would you believe she still wets her bed sometimes? At this age. And she demands so much attention. Constantly. It's like she wants us to follow her around like a cheerleading squad. I certainly didn't do that when I was young. You know how it was, when we were kids, we just got on with things. Maybe it's generational. But it gets so that I can't stand to be in the same room as her. Would you say that is normal?'

The old man coughed again and put his pipe into the ashtray. 'Water,' he said, 'could I have a glass of water?'

My father went to the kitchen to fetch him one and when he returned with it the older man was already on his feet, insisting that he was now fine, that he had enjoyed the evening very much. 'Good night,' he said, calling for his wife and moving quickly toward the door.

When they were gone, my father lowered himself back into his chair. I peeked out again and saw he had a thoughtful look on his face, like he was pleased by some new idea that had just occurred to him. Relighting his pipe, he stared for a long time straight ahead, hardly blinking, not moving, just pulsing his lips gently against the stem to release mouthfuls of smoke that gathered like fog around his head. The spiders in my lungs were in turmoil and it took all of my strength not to cough.

When eventually he tapped his pipe out in the ashtray and set it aside, he noticed the candle. I watched as he moved his fingers slowly, very slowly, through the flame. He started with his thumb and went through them all until he ended with his pinky. Flame on flesh looks like wax, like something that can melt away to nothing. In the fire his fingers glowed a beastly orange and I wondered how it was that he could stand the pain. When he was done, when he had worked every one of his fingers through the flame, he leaned forward and pinched it out.

＝

It's harder this time. I put the candle in the soda-can lantern, and sit again in front of the painting. My body is unwilling and it seems to remake itself around this reluctance. Other parts of the body don't protrude like the ear, and flesh doesn't lend itself willingly to the flame. My neck, especially, that pale concavity of skin, is tricky. And my hips, for some reason, my hips are reluctant to take. But I work through the night and in the end the pain is correct. When I lay on the hard floor next to my bed, matches, candles, and lighters scattered around me, I hear emanating from my own mouth the same low moan that came out of Conestoga, coarse with pain and fear, and I know the empty street of me has been perfectly razed.

16 Days

She walks the seams of the city, finding currents old and new. Coral stone archways embedded with sea shells, lamps flickering in the dark. She reads time in both clock faces and human faces, and the faces sometimes in the sky. Her mother and father are there because they are always there, cased in the machinery of her thoughts. She vomits in buckets and her father crushes a goat a thousand times. The stars above are perfect teeth, and everyone she sees stands on the blackest of hooves. Sometimes the sky is the sea and there is a figure coming out of the waves because he is lonely and there is something in loneliness that is like hope.

Her skin weeps. There are sixteen days until the end of time, and she is racked with pain. There is Green Jack on his corner, spreading rumors of redemption and grace. His words catch in the night like fishhooks. People jeer. She burns in her skin, has always burned in her skin, from ear to heel – all of her sharp now with the knowledge of what she has done. But what has she done?

Two paths to take from here and both reek of paint. Murals on walls, some done, some half done: fish launching themselves into the open nets of fishermen, girls in red-and-gold jellabiya waving to dhows in the distance, Arabian horses plunging across the sand. One of them, one of the horses, is blood red at the wide-open nostrils. She can see into his body through this portal, follow paths on paths that lead to places that shouldn't be seen. She can feel heels in her side, feel metal in her mouth. There is always a breaking. Sinjin drunk at the party. The way Liam leered, the way Abdullah was sad, the way he is always sad, and the falcon spinning its head looking for a way out. There is no more new god, no more tourists begging to be taken to the water chamber site, only the same old dusty lots telling the same story of a past that is dead and gone. She knows different. She knows the way it wakes and pulls itself free. She knows the way it sounds like something new moving through the streets.

She thinks that she passes herself on the street, one tall ugly girl covered in scalded skin, and she twists around, spiraling into herself, to catch sight of whatever it was she just saw. She licks her lips and tastes salt. And still Green Jack is talking. Still he is here on this corner even as he was on the other corner.

'We only know the surface of everything,' he says, 'we only know the finest breath of tissue that is this life. There are veins beneath our veins connecting us to every sea, to the very foundation of this world.'

She *thinks* barzakh and Green Jack *says* 'barzakh.'

'There are seas that exist in the darkest sky,' he says, his voice trailing up to the dark vault of clouds. He sees her and she sees him and he says that she has stepped through flame and she says that yes, she has. He lifts his hand to his heart and bows.

15 Days

It is Larvad who tells me she is dead.

I am in line waiting for food, everything smelling of

onions and the insect spray Badal is using in the bathroom. I watch him empty a can in there, he keeps the door open, apologizing for the fumes. His English is getting better. His shoulders have changed position – they've dropped from up around his ears – and he seems taller. He empties the spray can at the baseboards around the toilet. Makes himself cough. Makes us all cough. A few customers get up and leave. One doesn't even bother paying his check.

Larvad shouts after him, but then notices me and comes out of the kitchen. I think he's going to throw me out again, tell me to take my ugly ear and my knife and go somewhere else, but instead he tells me that she is dead.

'Hurry,' he says. 'Go right now. Run.'

The streets are still slick with the rain that fell during the day while I was sleeping. Everything is black and wet, and the mosque is far. Traffic is heavy, everyone seems angry and on edge, as if a thousand arguments have raged across the city. Running beneath a balcony something crashes just behind me. An egg, someone has dropped an egg. I keep running.

By the time I reach the mosque, which is small and flanked by a parking lot and a cemetery, I think there will be no one left, and that I will have missed everything. But there is a cleaner sweeping the front steps – a young man wearing boots that are too big for him. They clump and slide as he walks me to the front door. I'm about to go inside when he says madam, no, and points to my hair. I tell him I didn't bring a scarf, but I have to go inside. My voice is shaking. I cannot seem to catch my breath. The cleaner looks uneasy, holding his broom in both hands, chewing his lip. No English, he says. No Hindi, I say. We stare at each other for a moment. He is younger than me, just a boy with a broom and boots meant for a much bigger man. Then he lifts his hand, telling me to wait, and goes inside.

He is gone for so long I think he has forgotten me, that I have been left on the steps, but finally the big doors swing open and he comes out again, carrying a spare black scarf. Once I wrap it around my hair, he leads me inside and points toward the women's room.

Malak is alone. Her hijab has come undone, and one end of it is puddled in her lap where she is pulling the delicate threads apart one by one.

'Allah yirhama,' I say, my voice still shaking.

She does not look up. 'I tried to call you.'

I remember a ringing phone. I was asleep and the sound was shrill, and coiled so tight that I thought it came from within me, from the new burns on my skin.

'I'm so sorry,' I say. And then I say it again, thinking that maybe I should just keep on repeating myself, rushing out a torrent of apology until I am certain that Malak understands. I want to explain everything by telling her about the way Conestoga looked beneath all of his bandages, and about the way I can hear the sharp rattle of hooves even now, and about how, when the candle's flame reached the nape of my neck, it felt like the fire was working its way inside of me, finding new paths to take in my changing body. But then I see how small Malak looks sitting on the long wooden bench along the back wall – it is so tall that her short legs barely touch the ground. She is an orphan now, and in this empty room with its tall ceiling, she looks it. I sit beside her.

At my feet, I notice a small blonde head with a plastic smile. Someone has left behind a Barbie doll. She wears a wedding dress of white lace and sparkling rhinestones. In her hair, there is a single blue flower.

'Yesterday she ate a bowl of lentil soup and today she is dead,' Malak says. 'How do you eat a bowl of soup and then be dead? She asked for extra lemon, but we didn't have any and I didn't want to go back out to the shop. I told her I would get some for her today.'

There is a small table set up in the corner with an electric kettle and boxes of tea. I see a plate of cookies, a bowl of chocolates. I ask Malak if I can get her anything. She says no. She tells me she was supposed to leave hours ago.

'She bled. When I was washing her. Her body, I mean. Her body bled when I was washing it. From a sore on her heel. I didn't know that could happen.' Malak lifts her hands to her face and takes a deep breath. 'I still smell like rose water.'

She returns to her shawl and pulls free an entire black thread, which frazzles in its sudden freedom, crinkling up at both ends. She drops it on the floor and begins working on another.

'I should have been here,' I say.

'Yes. You should have.'

'Did I tell you she spat on me? After the accident.'

'To get rid of the 'ayn. She told me she wasn't sure if it would work, though. There are other things you could do, she said, things with salt and herbs. She said you needed to be sure about it because a thing like that can linger.'

Malak finally looks up, and when she sees my face, her eyes go wide. 'What happened?'

I lift a hand and find that my scarf has slipped back, revealing my burned ear and the burned side of my neck.

I pull it back down and tug the fabric more tightly beneath my chin. I tell her nothing happened. An accident.

'See?' Malak says. 'She was right. These things do linger.'

'Maybe.'

'You know, she dreamed about you after the last time you visited. When we made her bedroom into a garden. She told me about it in the morning. Her dream. She said that you had to drive him into the sea.'

'What?'

'I don't know. I didn't understand it. I thought maybe you would. What did you talk to her about that night?'

'I don't remember,' I lie. Drive him into the sea? The idea is absurd. I haven't even seen the sea, fully seen the sea, in years. And even here, sitting in this room on this worn bench with Bride Barbie and Malak unthreading her scarf, the sea feels perilously close.

'She was upset about the dream,' Malak continues. 'She kept trying to cover her eyes like there was something there that she didn't want to see. It must have been terrible.'

'I think we're all having terrible dreams lately.'

Malak surprises me with a grim smile. 'It is the end of the world, after all.'

There is a knock. Without opening the door, the cleaner with the too-big boots clears his throat, says madam, and we know it is time for us to leave. Malak rewraps her scarf over her hair. Noticing the discarded Barbie, she picks it up, straightens its gossamer dress, and leaves the doll to sit alone on the bench and watch us as we go.

Standing on the steps outside, Malak looks out at the dark graveyard. There are no lights, and the space is a wash of black interrupted only by the grey trunks of palm trees and small white huddles of piled stone. As a woman, Malak did not attend the gravesite for the burial of her mother, but she tells me that she watched carefully from the window and she knows where her body is.

'Do you want to go see it?'

'Yes.'

The grave of Um Malak is a low hillock of stones in the gritty sand beneath a slender palm tree. It doesn't seem possible that Um Malak is really here. If we hauled away the stones and moved aside the sand, I think we would find an empty space, a worn-out hollow in the ground with no body inside. I keep thinking that if she is in there, *really* in there, then she can't breathe. I feel breathless myself imagining it, worrying about the body where she used to live. I think about how I disturbed the last days of her life by telling her about Al Ghareeb, about the way he troubled her final dreams, and I wish I could take it all back.

Malak pauses at the end of the grave. She crosses her arms and takes several heavy breaths. I wait for her to cry but she does not. She just sways, like she is being buffeted by a wind that no one else can feel, and closes her eyes.

14 Days

When I finally found a place to live – after my father told me I had to leave – and felt able to venture outside again, all I did was walk. I walked until the streets lived in my bones, but I always turned back before I reached the edge of the souq so I did not have to confront the water. The sea was no longer something I could approach.

Walking, I learned more about the streets than I knew it was possible to know: I learned the cadences of the hawkers – when they were loud and when they were soft, when they beguiled and when they chided; I saw the lineages of the street cats – the calicoes in the northern blocks, the mottled gingers in the south, the lean black-and-whites with the pale green eyes in the east; near the Madkhal, I watched the taxi drivers waging their wars upon one another – the punctured tires, the soaped windshields, and the rides stolen by whoever had the quickest gas pedal; on Muthaf Avenue, I watched them build three museums right in a row; and, down near the Post Office, I watched the children battle one another with bottlecaps and dates, trading insults and jeers.

And now I walk with my hand on my knife and Um Malak's words in my ears: drive him into the sea. My body is terrible with pain, but still I walk, because what Al Ghareeb did to Conestoga, what I think maybe *I* did to Conestoga, won't be the end of things. An abomination does not stop until it is made to stop.

I tell myself I am not afraid because all time is now, which means I have already done this. He is already defeated; I have already driven him into the sea. I walk these streets and study them. I understand the flows of bodies, the way they maneuver themselves toward and away from the places there are to be. I look in their faces like I never look in their faces, at their eyes and their mouths and the way they comb their hair. I can see him, traces of him, in all things. Everywhere I go, he has already been.

13 Days

The carolers' candles blow out in the wind. The choir director, a short woman with a mountain range for a bosom, abandons her conducting and rushes to the children with the guttered candles brandishing her lighter.

'Cup your hand around it! Not like that, around it. No, *around* it!'

Some in the audience smile. Others pass by shaking their head, not liking that Christmas carols are being sung on the street – it isn't right. The children are wearing red and green sweaters and a few of them have Santa hats on their heads. One little girl in the front row doesn't sing at all, just blinks dazzled eyes at the audience and blushes when they clap. When the carolers finish 'Silent Night', the sound of the traffic fills in the sudden quiet – shrill horns protesting the slow-down at the roundabout from the road work being done. Sometimes the sound of a jackhammer.

Across the street, Shockwave Electronics is full of shoppers. I watch a customer argue with the clerk. He is pointing at something, the veins on his neck bulging, but the clerk just shakes his head and moves on to someone else. The clock in the window says *13 Days*, and the red glow of it flickers over the face of whoever walks by. The carolers begin another song, 'In the Bleak Midwinter'. Their voices tremble over the notes in the line, 'Earth stood hard as iron, water like a stone,' and I turn and walk away.

The man who argued with the Shockwave Electronics clerk is ahead of me on the sidewalk. I can hear him muttering. He dips in and out of English. 'Fucking idiot,' he says, 'fucking-stupid-stealing idiot.' I can see his feet, in sandals despite the cold, are cracked at the heel. He takes big steps, arms swinging, pulling me along in his furious wake. I coast behind him in the space he punches open through the crowd. I am thinking of earth hard as iron and water like a stone as he shouts: 'Thief, mad fucking thief!'

We reach the Madkhal and out he goes toward the sea, going where I cannot go, seeing what I cannot see, leaving me behind. Coming the other way, under the archway into the souq, is Green Jack, his coat flapping open at his sides like shabby wings. He walks with his head down, his shoulders hunched. I ask Green Jack where he's going and he looks up and smiles and tells me, 'Everywhere. I'm going everywhere. The question,' he says, slipping back into the crowd, 'is where are *you* going?'

I wait, leaning against the cool shoulder of the Madkhal, looking at the mural that is being redone. I think of the rogue painters – this must be their work. At one end is a scene of a peaceful beach, lancing palm trees, gentle waves, but it shifts in the middle, light emerging from the greenery of the palms to reveal the sinuous outline of bodies, maybe dancing, maybe doing other things. They have painted a moon overhead that dribbles down the sky, not a coherent thing at all, but a drooling bubble of cream. There are men here now in overalls rolling white paint over it all. They work with no passion. Slowly, carelessly, taking breaks for cigarettes and tea. While I watch they only manage to cover one palm.

I can feel, standing here and not moving, an alien pulse start up within the burn at my jawline. This burn is the deepest, most livid one on my body. When I looked at it in the mirror this evening, I saw a seeping red mouth and I wondered if it could speak, and, if it could, what it would say. The pulse within it is not the pulse of anything else – it isn't my heartbeat and it isn't my breath. It lives in its own time and keeps its own vision. Clarity. The pain of the burn is clarity. When people passing by see my face, they grimace. No longer do I feel like I am always hiding. All of this broken skin is letting me fall out from every direction – the thing inside me that has been building and building is beginning to leak. Like Green Jack, I'm going everywhere.

There comes a moment when the night falls under a hush: the roadwork pauses, the traffic slides by quietly, and the crowd, as one, takes a breath. All is quiet, all is calm, and into this moment of peace Al Ghareeb appears.

He is walking towards me, surrounded on all sides by people who do not seem to understand what is in their midst. How easily he moves through them, with his hands in the pockets of his coat, his collar turned up against the wind. I think of the carolers' candles blowing out and I feel myself flicker.

He is under the Madkhal now and still no one notices him, still he passes among them like he belongs to this life. I wait for him to notice me – he *must* – but he passes by without even looking my way.

I reach into my pocket and seal myself around my knife. The painters are painting, their white rollers blotting out their small private sky, rolling away the peaks of their waves, and Al Ghareeb says something to one of the painting crew as he makes it to the Madkhal's other side.

I follow him toward Shockwave Electronics where

he knocks on the window, and the clerk notices him and waves. When he passes the red glow of the apocalypse light, not a hint of it touches his face. We pass Larvad's, where I see Greta in the street jangling her waist pouch. '*Liebchen*,' she cries, '*liebchen*!' But I am already gone.

Al Ghareeb pulls a sprig of jasmine from a flower vendor's cart. The vendor shouts, 'You have to pay for that,' but Al Ghareeb just winks and tucks the bloom into his hair. We pass the school and the synagogue and the church, we pass the archeological site by my flat, and the karak stand that smells of cardamom and scalded milk. There are carolers here, too, another group, singing the same songs. Someone shouts at them to go home.

Al Ghareeb is walking fast, and I hurry to keep him in my sight. When I knock into people, I say excuse me, tell them to move, shove myself through the hard drift of their bodies. Al Ghareeb has a way of sliding through the tumult, finding the path of least resistance, that I cannot mimic. I watch him wind his thin body through a family, forcing a mother to let go of the hand of her child. We pass the carolers, these new children, singing about the earth that is hard as iron and water that is like a stone, and Al Ghareeb begins to move even more quickly, leaving me behind, so I break into a run.

But when I reach the intersection, Al Ghareeb is gone. I spin, wondering if he is inside a shop, if he has caught a taxi, or if he has simply vanished into another time. The crowd is wild here, a surge of holiday shoppers and tourists swinging cameras – everything is a face or a body or a voice.

And then I see him. Silver eyes in a pale face. Not gone at all. He is right here beside me.

I stumble back, yanking my knife from my pocket. Fingers slick and scrabble. I shout. I shout again. Words fall and break on the pavement. There is no sense.

Al Ghareeb watches me, standing unmoving while the crowd opens around him. Somehow, I am in the street. In my stumble I tripped off the curb. A car honks. A taxi driver shouts. Holding out my knife, I lunge toward Al Ghareeb. He smiles.

A woman carrying a cardboard box on her head appears between us. In the wind, her floral headscarf ripples across her face, but she does not lift a hand to stay it.

I dodge to the side, telling her to get out of my way, but Al Ghareeb is already gone. The space where he stood has filled with a child carrying a basketball, a woman using a cane, and a father holding a baby. The father rears away from me, clutching his baby more tightly to his chest. He has seen my knife. He looks into my face and there is fear in his eyes. So much of it. I put the knife back in my pocket, but, as I move down the sidewalk, I keep my fingers around the handle, waiting to pull it out again.

I look in the cold store. Inside, the shopkeeper is unloading a pallet of eggs into the chiller. He pulls a mottled brown egg from one of the cartons and lifts it to his face. A single feather dangles from the underside, white and curled, and he blows it to the floor and asks if I need help.

Into the next shop, a dishware and toy shop, where glass goblets share shelf space with cheap puzzles and stuffed animals, and the next, where washing machines and refrigerators gleam in orderly rows. He is nowhere. I move on down the street, fighting through the crowd, looking in every alley. I think I have lost him, I think I have failed, but then I see the long line of his outstretched leg. He has crossed the street. I follow.

Just as I am almost upon him, he turns and sees me coming. His head tilts to the side and it is so strange, so animalistic, like a cat assessing an injured bird, that I feel myself slow down to take it in. This is maybe not what I thought.

We face one another on the pavement and I think that now is the time I must speak, but then I notice his hands. He is rubbing his hands in front of him as if they are cold. He rubs them, rubs them, then pushes them down deep into his pockets. He licks his lips.

'Hello,' he says.

It is like looking into a mirror and hearing your own voice. Sight and sound mingle, crumbling against one another.

'Please.' My voice comes from a great distance, from another time where this has worked. 'You have to go.'

He frowns. From this close I can see that his eyelashes are so pale they are almost white.

'You have to go *now*.'

He turns away, I am losing my chance. A little girl flies by my legs, scattering a handful of leaves.

'You can't hurt anyone else.' My voice is louder now, reaching out to his quickly receding back. 'I know what you did. I know what you did!'

The little girl looks at me. Her eyes go round. She has seen my burn. I push her away and follow Al Ghareeb.

He cuts sideways through an alley and then darts across another street and around a corner and then—

The burned remnants of the Pyramid are gone.

The abandoned playground has been dragged clean.

There is no more bent jungle gym, no more leering slide, even the rocks and shrubs have been regimented, and look tidy and orderly, like a simulacrum of what an empty lot should be.

Al Ghareeb has brought me to the Milk Milk playground by a way that I did not expect. From this direction, there are no alleys for me to slip inside, and nothing for me to hide behind. I stand completely exposed as he walks through the dirt toward the half-finished mural that now covers the length of the building.

The mural is a ghost – pale lines of white paint tracing outlines of the scene to come. There is the rudimentary outline of waves and watery beams of light falling from a distant surface. A seabed scuttles with crabs and seaweed, and, far above at the surface of the water, there is a lean dark dhow. This is the only part of the mural that is finished. The dark wood of the boat looks like a hollow in the side of the building. The pearl diver leaping from the bow is a star falling from the sky.

Al Ghareeb walks slowly now, treading time the way a swimmer treads water. He does not look at the mural, but just stares at the ground, stepping carefully through the newly ordered dirt. He passes the mural and continues to walk along the perimeter of the lot. I edge forward, keeping my body flush against the side of the building. When I reach the middle, to my left I can see the ghostly white outline of what will someday be a sea snake. It coils in the water next to me, its mouth open and its fangs sharp.

'Don't move.'

While I was looking at the someday snake, Al Ghareeb was looking at me. He now stands in the center of the lot, the wind whipping his hair into a cloud.

I hold out my knife.

He lifts his hands, too. They are pale, bloodless and white.

'Leave,' I say. 'Leave now.'

'Don't move. You are in the right place.' His hands are now even higher. They shape a strange figure: forefinger and thumbs extended, the rest of the fingers curled into his palms. He angles them toward one another and lifts the square they make up to his face. Through the border of his hands, I can see more of him than I ever have before. There is a stillness to him, a sadness in his starlit eyes. I remember him hitting Conestoga, smacking him down into the street and leaving him there with his pain.

I step forward. My knife flashes. 'I know what you did,' I say. 'And I won't let you do it again. I won't let you do any more.'

A noise, a symptom of another time. He is laughing.

My hand is shaking now, my wrist, my arm, the whole of my body trembling like my bones are falling out of my skin. I tell myself to rush him, to scream, to wield the knife until he flees back to the waves he came from.

But I can't.

I just stand there against the ghostly mural, feeble knife in my hand, and watch as Al Ghareeb lifts his face up and up and up. He is looking at something far above my head now. His eyes narrow and his expression is thoughtful. Then he turns and walks away.

When he disappears around the corner at the end of the street, I fall to my knees. So close to the ground there is still the smell of something once living that was burned to its death, the dull green char rising from the place where the Pyramid once stood.

12 Days

She can feel the force of something, like wind, like waves, peeling up from her bones, reaching for whatever it is she is holding back. Her body aches from the burns and the run last night chasing her abomination. She remembers the way he walked so slowly through the playground, not caring about the corpses he was stepping over. She remembers the way she cringed against the wall next to the sea snake, letting him have his way because that is the only way. And then she remembers the way he lifted his head toward the cloud-quilted sky, looking up and up, taking stock of the building, and the way he had seen something within it. Now she knows. Flame on flesh and flesh on flame. They will be next.

11 Days

I do not know what I will say when I see them. It has been two years since we last spoke, since we have seen one another. There is the truth that is impossible, or there are lies that they would dismiss. A man from the waves is coming to kill you, and he carries in his veins my rage, this rage, this rage that you have always seen.

Thinking of standing in my father's doorway makes me feel as though my skin is being peeled away, and without it I fear I will fall into the sky, so I think of anything else.

There are streamers flapping from lamp posts, red and green and gold. It will soon be Christmas. There are posters in shop windows screaming about Y2K. It will soon be the end. By now, though, everyone is either prepared or unprepared; those who will make it through the coming apocalypse and those who will not. I wind down the hushed alleys of tailor shops and fabric stores where gauzy silk billows toward me and the tight bolts of cotton laid out next to one another look like ribs. Along the front of one shop there is a mural that makes me pause. A small goat stands against a tall dune, the desert sky huge as a cathedral overhead. There is nothing else in the scene, nothing but this goat that is caught in a pool of yellow light. Her small mouth has fallen open and inside the wet pink of it I see a glimmer of teeth. I tell myself it is nothing and keep walking.

I turn into the alley just behind Hollywood Video, where the air smells like fresh urine. When I come out the other side, there is the Milk Milk building. There is the scoured playground where Al Ghareeb faced me. There is the mural that is unfinished – the bobbing dhow and the ghostly possibilities of shark and fish and snakes. And there, on the third floor, is my father's flat. I tell myself I will take the stairs.

First, I walk through the playground, following the path Al Ghareeb took, looking down at my feet – which are just feet and not glossy sharp hooves – as they plume the dust into clouds. I don't walk across the burned footprint of the Pyramid – I find I cannot. Instead, I circle it, remembering the way it used to be, foliage fresh and green against the bulk of the building. I can feel my blood splashing around my heart, the tired heave of my lungs, even the moist hollows at the center of my bones.

The Pyramid. The place where I first gave voice to Al Ghareeb. Hiding in its dim interior with Malak and Hebah, Liam and Abdullah, and sometimes Sinjin, too. I did not speak much as a child, but that night I did. I felt like I had been waiting to speak for a very long time and, when I began my story, telling them about the strange creature I had seen coming from the waves, they all stopped to listen. Their faces were draped in shadow, green and serious, and my words ran from my throat. I leaned forward, pushing my knees into the rough gravel of the ground, explaining the mad emptiness that could drive a being to abandon the sea and take to land.

'He doesn't belong anywhere,' I said, repeating the phrase until I recognized the sad truth of it.

I spoke for what felt like whole nights of time, my words tripping over one another in their haste to leave my mouth. I didn't really finish, the story just roamed with Al Ghareeb on his clattering passage through the souq looking for a place to call home. I let him go on, but I stopped talking. The other children watched me, their eyes big in the dark space of the Pyramid's interior. Abdullah and Sinjin looked scared. Malak looked like she wanted to cry, but was holding herself very still to make sure she didn't. Hebah was crying. Her soft sobs were a small revelation in the crowded space. But Liam shook his head. Into the quiet he said, 'You're crazy.'

I could feel the tender weight of all of their eyes pressing into my face, into my skin, into the bones of my skull. It didn't matter that Liam was the one who said the words. It didn't matter *who* said it. It was the truth.

Now, the Pyramid is gone. Even the charred bits of wood have been cleared away, and the tracks they left when they dragged them off are still in the dirt. There are a few nails, here and there, that might have been part of the structure, used to hold it all together. I reach for one. Blow the sand off. Rub the rusty tip of it with the pad of my forefinger. Consider pushing it into my skin, letting it pierce apart some piece of me. But then I put it away in my pocket next to my knife and turn back to the building itself.

There is no way to approach the lobby of the Milk Milk building other than by the road that leads into the sea. The road where I first saw Al Ghareeb. The road where he first dragged himself up out of the waves and felt the earth against the underside of his hooves. The road I haven't stepped on in two years.

When I reach its very edge, I can smell the salt in the air. This smell isn't new to me; it isn't a surprise. I knew that I would have to face it. I tell myself that I don't even have to see the sea, which would have made this impossible. I can just keep my back to the water and enter the lobby, go up in the elevator, and into the flat, without ever once having to see it.

I face the building, imagining the elevator ride, the dissonant dings the carriage will make as we pass each floor, and how the carpet will still be the color of mustard – a yellow that reminds me of things like pus and hospitals and wounds that need suturing. The wounds on my leg. The pulse at my jaw. Even slower now than it was before. Something is winding down.

And then, after I knock, my father will be there at the door. My father, short and round with his hairless scalp and his eyes that are never anything but blank. He will not be surprised to see me, because nothing surprises him. He will just ask me what I want. I will hear nothing in his voice but time, and I will have to tell him that he was right about me. I have wrought an abomination.

I am backing away now, gasping for breath.

I was wrong.

There is no air.

Not this close to the sea.

10 Days

The carolers are on my street. They are standing on the pavement just below my window. I am woken by their songs. They sing that the earth is hard as iron and that water is like a stone, but they are wrong: water is never like a stone here; nothing freezes here. Here, water is only ever water. But still they sing of snow and frost and ice, as if all these things may come to pass. I open my window and look down upon them, letting the bite of the night air bother the burns on my face and the ones that stretch down my neck. The pulse in my jaw begins, knocking a different time to my heart, and I know that tonight Al Ghareeb is walking and I know that I will not face him.

Leaving the window open, I sit in front of the painting at the foot of my bed and tell myself that maybe it doesn't matter what Al Ghareeb does. Maybe I am simply in the permutation where abominations mete out their version of justice fueled by the rage of the one who dreamed them into being.

By the time I was in high school, my father and I hardly spoke to one another. Months would go by without a word. But there was a day when my mother was gone, traveling for an art exhibition, when he came into my bedroom. He didn't knock, would never have knocked on a door in his own house. I was not sleeping, but I did have my eyes closed. When he sat on the edge of my bed, my body turned in on itself, traveling through an interior that I had long cultivated, through a space that was a street that led elsewhere. The mattress sagged beneath him.

'Have I ever told you who you are?'

Opening my eyes, I shook my head.

'Nothing,' he said with a blank smile. 'You are nothing.'

This was how it went. Months of silence then a lecture, a transmission of knowledge that I was meant to accept without dissent. I held myself very still beneath my sheets and waited for more.

'You are nothing, I am nothing, no one is anything. Did you know that?'

I said that I didn't.

He got up and opened the window, letting in a hot wash of ocean air. He leaned there, his hands on the windowsill, looking out at the water. The water was the only thing that could be seen from my bedroom. The water in every direction. The side of the building dropped down sheer into the sea. Sometimes at night, during wild weather, the waves would hit so loudly along the bottom floor that I could hear them in my dreams.

My father always said he liked the way the building

was positioned, that it reminded him of Venice, and that we should enjoy it while it lasted, because land reclamation was soon to take the sea far away from us. But it never did. The road they built leading directly into the sea stayed unfinished, untouched by development, and so the Milk Milk building retained its watery perch.

The children in the building held fast to rumors that some older boys – at some point in a distant past that no one was quite sure of – had jumped off the roof of the building straight into the sea. We were divided on whether or not the boys had survived. 'The water at this part of the shore was much deeper in the past,' someone would say, 'it's gone shallow now, too shallow for jumping.' 'Not true,' someone else would say, 'it's still deep as anything. You could jump in there a thousand times and never die.'

When my father left the window, he came to sit back down on my bed. Not at the foot this time, closer to me.

'And do you know why we are all nothing?'

'No.'

'Do you want to know why?'

'Yes.'

'Because there is no self. Not in any of us. Nothing coherent and continual. Do you understand?'

I shook my head.

My father cleared his throat. 'Tell me who you were ten years ago.'

'Ten years ago, I was five.'

'And?'

'And I went to kindergarten. I played with dolls. I was on the soccer team. And I liked that cartoon. The one about the talking horses.'

'Alright,' my father replied. 'Are you like that now?'

'No, I guess not. I'm in high school. I don't play with dolls and I'm not on the soccer team.'

'And the cartoon?'

He was asking because he genuinely didn't know. I told him I didn't watch it anymore. That I hadn't watched it in years.

'Well, then.' He sounded pleased. 'What has stayed consistent within you? That self you described from a decade ago, that was so entirely you, that self that made up your entire world – where did it go? What is left of it?'

Through the window the ocean smelled rough, like things from the deep were being churned up and brought to the surface. 'Nothing,' I answered. 'Nothing at all.'

'Exactly.'

For a long time, he spoke. He told me about when he was a child – both the things he had loved, like collecting old army canteens and going camping, and the things he had hated, like waking up early and having to cook dinner for himself when his mother was gone and his father was at work. 'None of those things lasted,' he said, 'even though, at the time, I would have said they were a permanent fixture within me. I thought I knew who I was. But then I realized that there was no me to know. That's the great pleasure of life, learning to see the emptiness.' He poked me on the leg with a finger. Gave me a little shake. And smiled. 'I decided very early on that I wasn't going to play a role,' he went on. 'Not the way society tells you you should. Not husband, not father, nothing. I am completely free, unencumbered by anything.'

'And this makes you happy?'

He looked surprised that I had spoken. 'Well, now, there is no such thing as happy. No such thing as sad, either, when it gets right down to it. There is nothing at all. We are just the universe experiencing itself. Each of us are just a small part of the whole, briefly rising up to have this experience that we think of as *real*.'

The hot wind coming in off the water was so thick with humidity that it felt rough on my skin, like someone was dragging their calloused fingers all over my face. 'Did you think these things when you were young?' I asked. 'When your mother was crazy?'

For a long time, he looked at the window, smiling, blinking, not speaking. He resembled his mother, I realized. Not the round face and upturned nose, but the eyes. There was something in the eyes that reminded me of her. She had a way of looking at the people she was with, as though she was seeing something beyond them. In him, it translated to a blankness, a faraway distance. I don't think I had noticed the similarity before because I never thought of my parents as people who had once been children with parents of their own; I had never thought of my father growing up with a mother who went so mad she forgot his name.

My father turned back toward me. He lifted his pointer finger and it stood up steady, there was nothing about him that was trembling. 'I have,' he said, 'only one thing to say about all of that: the past can only affect you if you let it.'

'But you told me that all time is now. That's what you said. Which means that the past isn't ever really over. It's happening to us even now.'

He got up and moved to the doorway, standing there in the shadow, and I saw something flicker in his eyes – for a brief moment they were no longer empty. There was something there. He was breathing heavily and, suddenly,

I wanted to take back what I said. I leaned forward and reached out, as if I could find the sentence somewhere in the air around me and pull it all back into my mouth.

He left without saying another word.

It wasn't until later that evening – after the sun had set and the wash of rough, hot sea air had died away – that I recognized what I had seen in his eyes. The small swimming vision I had seen rising to the surface of his gaze, filling up the space that had all my life been blank, was something I recognized well. It was fear.

In my flat, sitting in front of the painting, I pull from my pocket the nail that I plucked from the Milk Milk playground. With the nail I trace the contours of the couch, following the arms, the cushions, the back. There are ridges in places where the paint is thick, where my mother let it rise up to achieve texture and depth, and there are places where the nail slides quick and smooth, places where she was loose with her brush to create motion. I make space for myself, weaving the tip of the nail clear around my form. I wonder if I should slice my figure out entirely. Maybe the painting was always meant to be empty of me.

The memories that come back to me are always terrible. Above all, what I remember is foul and bogged down with feelings of guilt and panic and rage. But there are other memories. I know there are others. Sometimes, I remember them, too. There were the days when my father took me to the desert to look for shark teeth. And the days he brought me home books from the library simply because he knew I would like them. Or when he told me I was wise beyond my years, when he said I could do anything I wanted to do. And there are the memories of my mother. The birthdays that were an embarrassment of gifts, the Christmases when she baked every kind of cookie, and the Halloweens when she would hand-make my costumes, which were always the best in my class. She carried her video camera everywhere, bulky and too big on her narrow shoulder, always training its black eye on me, saying she didn't want to forget a single thing.

These memories are good, but they are small, and they wield less gravity than the others. As if fewer things are drawn into their orbit. I wonder what is wrong with me that I remember my life like this, in bursts of pain and fear.

I drag the nail faster and faster, thinking of all the things Al Ghareeb could do. When I push the sharp tip into the surface of the painting, piercing the canvas, the paint around the puncture splinters. Pieces of it – the grey of a shadow, the green of the sofa – flake off and fall to the floor. At my feet, all around me, are pigments of the past.

9 Days

At Al Hadiqa there is a small circle of people, their backs lined up like fingers in prayer. I push my way into the huddle to see what they are looking at. It is a dead kitten. The thing was too new to have ever even opened its eyes.

'Are there others?' someone asks. 'Should we look for them and help?'

'If there are, its better if we let them die now.'

A young woman with a withered arm reaches forward to pluck the kitten from the ground. Its small white head lolls. She says she will not leave it there like it was nothing.

I go into Malak's building and knock on her front door. For a moment I think I hear something inside, the sound of the television, or the slide of the balcony door being pulled open, but no one comes. I bang on the door, heaving my body against it, calling out for her, calling even for Um Malak, before I remember that she is dead and buried beneath white rocks in a graveyard full of bodies.

A door down the hall flies open. Mr Milo, Malak's neighbor who moved back to Bangladesh, sticks his head out and tells me to be quiet, people are trying to sleep.

'But you're gone,' I say. 'You left.'

'Well, I'm back,' he answers with a scowl.

'Where are they? Where is she? Malak.'

'Gone. They're both gone. One dead and the other just gone.'

'Gone where?'

'Well, that is for God to say.'

'Not Um Malak. Malak. The daughter.'

'She left. That's all I know. Suitcases and boxes and now she's gone.'

'You saw her? When?'

'This morning. She got into a taxi.'

'Where did she go?'

He laughs as he shuts his door. 'How should I know that?'

8 Days

The alley behind Escape Now stinks. Something died here not long ago, a cat or a dog. A monkey, maybe. It's a ripe smell, the smell of a body being broken down. I have carried in my arms a cardboard box of glossy travel brochures from the file room. The box is heavy and my grip is slipping. Taking a quick step forward, I heave it into the big blue dumpster. It lands like a sack of meat and cities spill out – Paris and London and Kuala Lumpur and Istanbul and Antwerp and Nairobi.

From inside the dumpster comes the sound of things scurrying, I've woken something up. Rats, maybe. I tell myself it is a whole city of rats in the dumpster, rats who know their streets and know their time. The brochures have landed on top of them and I imagine I've brought down chaos and brimstone from the sky. Death from above – what a marvel I am.

From my pocket I pull out a lighter and the flame springs to life with the first flick of my thumb. I lean over the dumpster and set the corner of a brochure alight. The flame spreads quickly, as if things in this dumpster have just been waiting to burn. The fire licks across a sheaf of old newspaper, smoke roils across old palm leaves, and a magazine with the face of a Bollywood star on the cover curls up and turns to ash. The destination brochures are vanishing, which makes me think of Malak and where she might be. As the fire grows bigger, swallowing more and more, I step away from the heat and watch the smoke rise. I wonder if Al Ghareeb has emerged from his water. I wonder if he can see what I've done.

The scurrying intensifies, and then, from the back of the skip, I see a dark clotted river burst free. Rats pouring away to safety. I wonder if I've killed any of them, if any nests of pink hairless babies are being cooked to jelly beneath my flames. I decide I have; I won't pretend this was a bloodless act. This is a time for doing monstrous things.

7 Days

In my dreams, my mother and my father.

6 Days

There is a single street.

5 Days

And this is where it ends.

4 Days

The city block leading to the water chamber site is covered in murals that show a single life. The first panel reveals a small brown seashell of an infant surrounded by billowing white shapes that might be cloth and might be clouds. At the edge of this mural, yellow light ripples toward the child, as if he is being held up by the sun itself. On the next panel, wedged awkwardly between an auto shop and a small warehouse, the infant has become a small boy. He is running on lean legs that pummel the earth of a palm grove, the trees have been caught mid sway, bowing over him like protective arms shielding him from a too-blue sky. There is a green parrot in the upper right corner, a streak of green buzzing overhead. Its tail fizzles like a falling missile. The next panel shows the boy, now a lanky teenager, crouched near a campfire in the desert. Overhead, the smoke from the fire smears the dark sky. All around him, empty dunes. I think he is alone, until I see, painted very small along the twisted lip of the most distant dune, a stippling of black hoofprints. Subsequent murals show him as an adult fishing from a small boat, with grey hair as he rides a horse, as an old man facing the street, eyes wide open, laughing. In none of the murals is there anyone else, only this one life moving through time.

In the last mural, painted over the side wall of a cold store, the now old man, hunched and using a cane, stands before two open doors. One door reveals a vista of cold stars. The other door opens onto a profusion of light, a dense wall of it so fierce that nothing else can be seen beyond. The light is the same clear yellow that lapped the edges of the first mural, when this old man was just a swirl of an infant.

I leave the row of murals behind. At the gate for the water chamber, I ask the guard if I can see Elias. I tell him I was invited, worrying that he will tell me no, go away, and that he won't swing open the gate. But he is reading a magazine with a red sports car on the cover and he doesn't even look at me as he hauls open the iron gate and waves me through. I tell him I don't know where to go, but he's already back in his booth, head down over his pages.

The site is a wide walled lot at the far end of the souq, which is so thick with palms that in some places I cannot see the night sky above. I walk the winding path toward a small trailer that I can see at the far wall, passing low stone structures and open dig sites. There is a yard around the trailer, with flower beds full of purple and yellow pansies that have seen better days. Some of their heads have been lopped off, and the rest are bedraggled, splattered with mud. To one side of the trailer's short metal stairs there is a pile of cardboard boxes and an overflowing trash bag. Loose papers flap in the wind, and when I knock on the flimsy door there is a shout:

'I told you, just bring them inside! The door is open.'

I push the door open into a narrow room, with a dusty sofa, a television set, and a dining-room table with only three legs. The missing leg has been replaced with a stack of yellowing newspapers. On the walls, there are calendars from years long gone, open to show still-life depictions of rotting fruit and dying flowers. In the kitchen, propped up with an empty carton of milk, I see the painting of my mother. Doomsday nipples leer in the gloom.

'Did you find them?' Elias appears from a hallway holding an armful of clothes. He is wearing a tattered shirt that is buttoned up wrong, cargo pants, and, on his feet, thick winter socks. 'Oh. I thought you were Tarik. I told him we need more boxes. The ones we have are shit.'

He empties his arms over a suitcase, and says that, if I have come for the tour he offered, it is too late. 'As you can see, I am on the way out.'

'Is she going too?' I feel relief, thinking that maybe my mother will slip Al Ghareeb's grasp.

Elias is leaning over the suitcase, shoving things into pockets and, when he looks up at me, I can see that his eyes are bloodshot.

'You still don't know?'

'Know what?'

'About your mother.'

'What about her?'

'Your mother and me. Or,' he snorts, 'your mother and your father, I suppose I should say now.'

'What happened?'

'Your mother happened. Doesn't she always? She left me. Went back to your father.'

I sit down heavily on the chair by the front door. Plastic, rickety, it tilts me to one side and I have to put my foot out to stop myself from falling. 'When?'

'A month. Or two. I don't know. Time is a bitch, isn't it? She said she wrote you a letter. Or she said she *would* write you a letter. I can't remember.'

I think of the putty-pink envelope beneath my bed and the arm of my flimsy chair buckles.

Elias is packing books now, shoving them into a cardboard box that has been labeled and relabeled many times. In red marker on one side I can see the phrase: *Delicates! Warning!*

'We were at school together in Beirut,' he says. 'Do you know Beirut?'

He doesn't wait for me to answer before continuing.

'Before the war, ah, before the war, Beirut was the center of the world, wasn't it? The skiing, the beaches, the food. And the girls. The women. Your mother was always the most charming. That laugh…'

My leg starts to shake, and then my foot slips, shooting out across the trailer's slick floor.

'Do you know your father never asked her to come back?' He crashes an encyclopedia into the box. 'Never picked up the phone, never wrote her a letter, never made a single move to take her from me. And still, she goes back to him. I asked her what I had done wrong, what I had done to make her leave, and she told me that I was only a memory to her, and it turned out that a memory was not something on which to build a life. But we *did* build a life, I told her. For two fucking years.'

He pulls the top of the box together so roughly that a corner of it tears. For a moment, he stares down at the box, and then he shoves the whole thing off the table and the books thunder to the floor. One of them, *An Illustrated Guide to the Babylonians*, skitters toward me. When I reach for it, the legs of my chair splay out and tip me over.

Elias turns, finds me getting up from the floor, and asks if I want to see it.

'See what?'

'What you came here for.'

He throws open the front door of the trailer, and his feet, going down the metal steps, sound like gunshots.

I follow him to the edge of the yard, where there is a tall metal pole. Reaching into a control panel, he hits a bank of switches, and suddenly there is light. From floodlights at every corner, the site is illuminated.

'Ready?' he asks, walking away before I can answer.

The water chamber sits alone at the center of the site. The trees, the other structures, even the path, hesitate to approach. The ground beneath our feet, halfway there, gives way to a muddle of packed dirt and loose gravel. Elias tells me to watch myself – and, really, we should have flashlights. 'But fuck it,' he says, walking fast. 'Fuck it.'

The stairs leading down into the earth are wide and smooth and bowed in the middle from the footsteps of people long dead.

'Four thousand years, give or take,' Elias says when I ask him how old it is.

When my head slips below ground level, and I am encased beneath the earth, I think to myself that I have been swallowed by time itself. There is the smell of old water and mildew, the echo of everything. We reach the bottom of the steps and the only light is that which falls in from the floodlights at the surface, far away at the very top of the stairs. My eyes adjust to the darkness and I can just make out walls white as bone and a gleaming ripple of water.

'The ancients believed that by submerging themselves in this water they were honoring their god of water, who was also the god of chaos,' Elias says. His voice is quieter down here so far from the surface. 'They thought they were showing their willingness to put themselves in his hands, as it were.'

My whole body goes taut with a sudden yearning and

I step forward, but Elias says no. Don't go any further. The ground is too slick, I could fall.

We listen to the drips of condensation and the foggy sound of our own breath. Elias, I realize, never put on any shoes. The stone must be cold against his feet, which are just in socks, but he simply stands next to me, head jutting forward, staring unblinking into the darkness.

'Why did you lie about the new god?' I ask.

He is quiet for so long that I think he is not going to answer. But then he speaks, slowly, finding his words as he goes.

'I wasn't lying, at first,' he says. 'I believed I was right. I just went about things the wrong way. And, looking back, I can see that it took me too long to admit I was mistaken. I just kept thinking I could make it alright. Thinking things could be different. I don't know. Maybe I just wanted something too badly.'

From out of the corner of my eye I think I can see his shoulders shaking and I wonder if he is crying.

'There were days when I was doing this work when I felt like I was ahead of myself,' he continues. 'I'd find that things had already happened because I'd done them and it was like I had to catch up.'

'My friend,' I say, 'thinks time is going weird because the world is about to end.'

At this Elias laughs. 'People throughout history have always thought the world was ending. Mind you, many civilizations didn't greet this with mass panic and hysteria. They weren't like we are today. They had myths and legends that helped them navigate time. To them, the end was merely the beginning of another cycle. The end was a time to be reborn.'

'Is that why people came down here to the water chamber? To be reborn?'

Elias shrugs. 'Anything is possible.'

When we surface, there is a trace of dust in the air, and Elias tells me a shamal is coming. He can smell these things when they are still days away, he explains, and this one has been building for a while. He tells me it is going to be very bad. I look to the sky and see a pale grey ring around the moon, dust high up in the atmosphere, caught in the stars.

'I need to ask you for something,' I say. 'I need a favor.'

We reach the trailer and Elias hits the light switches, plunging us back into darkness.

'Please can you tell my mother to be careful,' I continue. 'Both of them. My father, too. They both need to be careful.'

'Why?'

'I can't explain. Please just tell me you'll do it.'

'I'm leaving. I'm not going to see her again.' His voice is heavy. He is already gone.

'Call her then. They have to know.'

'Why can't you do it?'

'I just can't. I can't speak to them. I tried.'

'You haven't seen her at all these last two years.' He is not asking a question; he is stating a fact.

'Neither of them.'

He sighs. 'I'll call her before I leave in the morning. But what am I supposed to say? Be careful about what?'

I think of his false god and my abomination, and for a moment I almost tell him everything because I think he might understand the way the past can fold in on itself. But

I can see the exhaustion on his face, and I know it is time for me to go.

'Tell them that someone might be trying to hurt them.'

'What? Who?'

'It doesn't matter. Just call her.'

'Have you told the police?'

'I have to go.'

I turn away, making for the path into the palms, but just before I reach it, he calls out.

'She always said you were crazy,' he says, and his voice is solid in the quiet night.

When I get home, I lower myself to the floor and snake my arms beneath my bed. Following a sticky river of old spilled tea, I find the putty-pink envelope embedded beneath a dusty clump of hair and an old hairbrush. When I pull it out, I see that the spilled tea has warped one corner of it, curling it backward on itself like a dying beetle.

The letter opens how I knew it would open – with my mother telling me that it has been too long since we last saw one another. She says she misses me so very much.

You don't know a mother's love, she writes. *You shouldn't punish me like this. I'm not something to be taken for granted.* Each period at the end of every sentence is a fist driving through the page, so hard has she wielded her pen.

I thought you should know that your father and I are together again now. I know you will be happy to hear this. You should come see us. There are some boxes of your things still here, and I can give them to you then. We are both keeping busy. We heard about your accident and hope you're alright. The roads are very dangerous these days. Just the other day when I was driving home from the club, I hit a cat. Don't worry, I'm alright – but the poor cat isn't!!

The dots of the two exclamation points illustrate the eyes of a small cat. Below them she has drawn, in her competent hand, the cat's grimly arching mouth, its lips peeled back in a hiss.

3 Days

The souq is in tatters. Christmas decorations flap in a wind that brings dust, and twinkle lights flicker and fade. Everything smells of wet paint. The murals have made people angry. They are not doing what they were supposed to do. They are too insidiously personal, it is being said – too much the vision of one man. He has remade the world and now we all feel like foreigners here. Coming out of a cold store I see a little boy crying, saying the monster scared him. Around the corner, I find a mural of an open grave, with a skeletal hand reaching out. From the shadows of the painted earth, I can see the faint sheen of something wet.

For a while, time passes without me. I walk in circles around Al Hadiqa as if that will make Malak appear, carrying her stool and her tattered pages of poetry. But she does not come to find me because she has left. And how strange it is to think of the souq as a place that *can* so easily be left.

Cutting through the foliage, I make for the edge of the souq, thinking of my parents and what will become of them. I wonder if they know by now that they are in danger.

I tell myself I have done enough. I wonder if I have done enough. I wonder if any of us have ever done enough.

When I find myself standing in front of Bait Azraq, I realize this is the only street that I have seen in the souq that is untouched by a mural. The blank walls here are dark with shadow. Bigger than all the rest of the buildings, Bait Azraq looks like an outcropping of ocean that has hauled itself onto land, blue and dark in the grim night that smells of the incoming shamal. I remember Um Malak's words to me about the night I ran from here in tears. Flickers of memory flare up and then fade.

And then the door of Bait Azraq swings open.

The sound of the rusty hinges makes me think of the cry of a frightened cat, high and shrill and sharp. I expect hooves, I expect a corona of wild hair, and my body is ready to run. But then there comes a ripple of a green cloak, dirty along the hem and threadbare at the shoulders. It is Green Jack and he is asking me if I would like to come in.

We dream our way through the cloistered spaces of Bait Azraq's courtyard, shielded from the wind and the dust and the terrors of the street. And, all the while, Green Jack talks to me about the things he needs me to know. I think we have been walking together for a very long time. His green tatters move like seaweed as he trails through gardens that are not dead, just wild. The bougainvillea is a bloody purple and the trailing jasmine is thick enough to hide a body. And the stage is still here, buckled and warped and shrouded in cobwebs.

'Nonsense places are thin and things can get through. All the way through! This place is so thin you can feel it in your teeth,' says Green Jack as he brings me through a wooden doorway into a narrow hall. There is a small lantern on the floor – inside a thin flame flickers.

Coming from somewhere, there is the sound of pigeons, a flock of them, cooing. The soft, quilted sound is vast, but no matter where I turn, I cannot find the birds. The sound lives in the air and I walk into it, pulling it down into the root system of my body. I ask Green Jack if he is really living here.

'Of course,' he answers. 'So are you.'

I do not remember the first time I saw Green Jack – he exists in my memory as far back as I do. Always in green and yellow, always with a beard that swallows his face, he was constantly on the street speaking to everyone and to no one. When I was very young, I used to believe that he was speaking to the buildings because they were the only ones who ever seemed to be listening.

Leading me up a staircase that trembles beneath our steps, Green Jack turns around and goes up backward, grinning at me. I wonder if he is planning to kill me. Some people say he is mad, that he is violent, but all he does now is keep on grinning at me and jabbing the tip of his very pink tongue at his gumline.

'You feel it here. *Here*. The thin places,' he says. 'Where things can get *through*.'

We go up the stairs for a thousand years and I watch myself age like the boy in the mural. I move through so many times that soon I know I will stand before two very different doors. All I can think of is the yellow light.

'Look,' says Green Jack, finally coming to a stop.

He has brought me up to the rafters that crisscross above the stage. These walkways of wood and rope are where the puppeteers used to do their work. On some of them there are piles of bright cloth – old puppets that have been left behind.

'Wait here,' Green Jack says, before he scrambles out onto a wooden walkway that crosses the whole of the long stage. There is no body beneath his tatters, I realize; there is nothing to see that is human. He vanishes into the far wing.

I wait for a long time, listening to the deep, throaty hum of the somewhere-pigeons. How stupid I am for following this strange man into this strange place. No one knows who Green Jack is or even where he comes from: he speaks any language you care to ask him about and does so, apparently, without an accent. He doesn't even have a job that anyone knows of, and he never seems to live anywhere for very long.

And then there comes, from the rafters on the other side of the stage, a falling body. It spirals like it is peeling itself apart in midair, legs and hair and face pinwheeling around and around. In the strange half-light I can see glossy eyes, floppy ears, and a row of perfect teeth. When it hits the warped wood of the stage, the body makes a thundering clatter that sounds like hooves.

Suddenly, I remember.

Um Malak had said that it was the dead body of the goat flying down from the rafters that made me cry. But she was wrong. In the play, Juha only *tried* to kill the goat. He tried to kill it any way he could think of – running it through with a sword, knocking it in the head with a boulder, pushing it off a mountain. But the goat would not die. No matter how many terrible things were inflicted upon it, it always got to its hooves still living. At this, the children around me in the audience roared with laughter – they guffawed and cackled and clapped. And it was *this* that made me cry.

Watching that play made me remember the body of the little goat beneath the wheels of our car. The perfect teeth in its skinless head and the sad rolling eyes. I had cried because it was all my doing. Now, and in the future and in the past, it was me who would always make that goat encounter its own death – again and again and again.

Now, from the other side of the stage, Green Jack screams: 'Thin places! Things can get out! Things are born every day but there was something born right here! And it found the way out!'

The air around us begins to shudder, filling with a pulse that matches the one in my jaw. A thousand wings battle the darkness as the flock of somewhere-pigeons takes flight. They were, all this time, hidden in the rafters just over my head. They beat upward, funneling themselves into the courtyard and out toward freedom.

2 Days

By the time I came home from Bait Azraq, I thought Green Jack had shown me everything; I thought I had remembered all there was to remember. But now, I see more. Now, I remember leaving the Bait Azraq of long ago with tears running down my face, with Um Malak shouting at me to come back. I ran all night, ran and ran, until I became every street of the souq.

When I finally returned home, the sun was rising. My parents said they had been panicked looking for me all night. Seeing them then, seeing that their fear was the same thing as their fury, I knew what would happen.

I was pushed into my bedroom. The sharp click of the lock on the outside of the door sounded like teeth snipping something apart.

When I woke later in the day, I watched the sun lower itself into the ocean. I waited for something to come from the merging of flame and liquid, but the sun was just swallowed up into nothing. I had to use the bathroom and I was thirsty. There were bottles of water beside my desk, and I told myself there would be enough. I drank one and waited. I knocked on the door, but there was silence in the apartment. I told myself not to think about food so I wouldn't get hungry. I watched the sea. I read a book and tried to ignore a situation that was becoming desperate. When a stinging wetness began to trickle from between my legs, I squatted over my trashcan, and listened to the spit of warm liquid against steel. When I finished, I wiped myself with a dirty sock and put the wastebasket in my closet, telling myself I wouldn't have to do that again. I watched the sea. I read another book. I tried to do homework, but I had left the worksheet I needed in the living room. I found a granola bar in my backpack and ate it. I knocked on the door again. I watched the sea. By the time the sun rose I had used the waste basket again. When daylight filled my bedroom, it made the stink coming from the closet stronger. I watched the sea. I knocked on the door. I drank another bottle of water. I watched the sea.

I found a coloring book and three crayons, so I colored. I brushed my hair. I tried to sleep. I watched the sea.

At sunset, I started to tell myself a story about the street leading into the water, and about the people who went in and the people who came out. Over the years, the road had crumbled, dropping huge rocks, huge pieces of itself into the waves. This, I decided is what made up the person I was beginning to see – a person made of the street itself. That was why, I understood, he could never settle. That was why he roamed and clattered himself around the city. He had hooves. He was capable of anything.

Just before my mother unlocked the door and let me out of my room, I watched this man made of rocks emerge from the sea. A strange man who was a stranger, Al Ghareeb. Watching from my bedroom window, my veins thirsty for the water I had already drunk, I saw him standing there at the place where the road fell into the waves. His spinning eyes were the silver of the stars and through them I could see the truth of time.

1 Day

I wake to a sick light. All is yellow and all is grim, everything charred with sand and dust that have traveled a thousand miles to poison our sky. I sit up and cough. My mouth tastes like I have spent the day chewing rocks. The shamal is on us and I am being watched. At the foot of the bed, the painting no longer looks like itself. There are scars running through the paint, rupturing the green sofa, the ugly curtains, and the long dark floor. The figure alone is untouched.

Pushing away my sheet, I look down at my arms, my legs, the spread of my belly, and I see scars and burns and lesions and scabs. Twists of skin so inflamed they must be infected. All along the edges of my body I burn and this is how I know the streets are open to me. It is time now for the end.

Fireworks go off when I make it outside, though it is not quite midnight. Wind tears down the narrow lanes, whipping trash into swirling eddies and plastering skirts and thobes to legs. No one can breathe. The crowd is a collection of knives, people drunk and ready, their eyes restless and eager. A woman jiggles by me, screeching with laughter as a man chases her. He claws at the air, and she screams louder. I watch him lunge for her waist, his fingers jabbing into her soft flesh. An old man at the corner claps and whistles. From every balcony, there are whipping streamers and loud music and the sound of children crying.

As I move through the souq, sweeping toward the east where everything will end, I see that all of the murals are finished. The world is in disguise. The walls are forest glades and stone-age huts and dunes covered with camels. There are paintings of women singing at the seashore with gold knots in their hair as their men coast home in boats made of mahogany. Everywhere there are pearls.

On the corner by the mosque, I find the tissue seller, and I watch her watching me pass by. When a firework booms overhead, I think I see behind her veil the darting shape of eyes. When I cross the street in front of Copper Top, I see a laughing Liam and Abdullah walking up the stairs, followed by Sinjin who is laughing most of all. His whole body shakes with it and his eyes are streaming with tears. Again and again the sky fills with cataclysmic explosions of green and blue and red and white. The sound is a premonition of the end: it is the splitting of the atom, it is the distance between the permutations. But, through it all, I keep walking. There is only one place he will be.

When I reach the Milk Milk building, I move through the picked-clean emptiness of what was once the playground, noticing a new path that has been cut through the very center. Just beyond the space where the Pyramid used to stand, I find that the ghostly mural has finally been completed. In the place where I stood just days ago to confront Al Ghareeb – pressed up against the wall holding my knife and shaking in my skin – a figure of a girl has appeared.

She is a pearl diver at the bottom of the sea. Her ruddy hair swirls out behind her and in one hand she holds a knife. In the other, an oyster. It is not opened yet, which means it may contain anything at all. Far overhead, the boats and the sun are in a different world. Down here, with the snake and the fish and the shark, the girl exists in the space between the salt water and the fresh; she will live forever in the barzakh.

A flash of motion.

It is Al Ghareeb walking down the crumbling road toward the sea. His whole body is angled forward: he has a destination this time, he knows where he needs to be.

I feel my body copy his, I feel myself tipping forward, I feel my feet clatter on the road. When the next firework booms in the stars, I catch my first sight of the sea.

In the darkness, there is no end to it. Not even the horizon. There is only the water, and there has only ever been the water. I am dizzy and then I feel a choking wave of nausea, saliva fills my mouth, my throat, so much that I think I will drown. I spit it into the wind, and it splatters me on the chest. I think of Um Malak and what she was willing to do to help me. I tell myself that Al Ghareeb isn't the only one who can move through time at will, and so I push myself forward, gagging every time I breathe in the sea air, gagging until my eyes stream and the pulse at my jaw is a red wall of pain.

But then I am inside the Milk Milk building. When the glass doors shut behind me, the stench of the sea vanishes and everything smells of old carpet and mildew. Al Ghareeb steps into the elevator; I take the stairs.

The yellow carpet in the hallway of my parent's floor is faded now, worn thin and dingy at the center. I wait outside their flat, wondering where Al Ghareeb could be. Is it possible he is already inside? I press my ear to the front door and listen. There is nothing but silence.

I check the doorknob and it twists in my hand. I enter silently and it is like stepping back in time. There is the framed pencil sketch of the Arabian oryx. On the coat rack there are my mother's abayas – the somber one of plain black silk and the one lined in silver sequins that glitter. Walking by the living room, I see the murky green couch. It looks so much smaller than I remember. But the room still smells of pipe smoke and the curtains fall in their same heavy folds to the floor. And there, on the side table, is a smudge of silver – the snuffbox. Further down the hall, I find that the bathroom door is open. I stare at the space between the toilet and the bathtub, and I see myself sitting there, a scared insect with her gas mask eyes, counting each turning page and every exhalation.

At the end of the hall, a light. My father is in his study as he often is at this hour – reading, grading papers, making lesson plans. I approach the door, careful to stay out of sight. Small behind his desk, I see his bald head inclined over a book. He has a cup of tea to one side and a blue pen to the other. His shoulders are round, and the sparse fringe of hair still remaining above his ears has more grey in it than before. But I know, if he were to look up and see me in the doorway, that his eyes would be the same as they ever were – they would glare and waver like flat stones at the bottom of a shallow pond.

He shifts in his seat and I move back. From this new angle I can see more clearly the bookshelf to my left. Perched atop the highest row of books are two clocks that I recognize. They each stopped at a different time. They passed their last seconds at different moments and will now forever live apart.

I think of the things I could say to my father. I could start with the monkey. Or the man in the hospital. Or the way the bed sagged when he told me I was nothing. Or the goat. The real one and then the puppet. I could tell him about the way it survived each and every way Juha tried his best to kill it.

Or maybe I would say that I can imagine the way he must have looked when he was young and alone, when his own mother forgot his name. And I could tell him that he was wrong. That I can see that now. Not about time, no, but about what the truth of time really means. But instead of saying anything I turn away.

Crossing the hall, I nudge open the door to my bedroom and find that here everything is different. All of the furniture I knew is gone, even the paint on the wall has been changed. The room is now an art studio, with canvases, shelves of paint, and tall easels crowding the space like a herd of nervous deer. The familiar smell of linseed oil and old paint floats into my face like a cloud.

And then I see my mother. The tall perfection of her is folded into a chair by the window. There is movement at her side – a pale rise of smoke circling up from an ashtray. Without looking away from the view, she reaches for the cigarette and brings it to her lips. I remember then the feel of her hand on my shirt when I tried to go toward her father in his nursing-room bed, her hand that pulled me back, held tight, and would not let me be touched by that danger.

Backing away to leave, I see her paintings. The canvases range in size and the paintings in states of completion, but every subject is the same. Each work is nothing but the sheer blue wash of ocean that she can see from this room. I recognize the angle of the horizon and the warp of light on the waves. She is painting the sea that I spent my childhood gazing into.

Al Ghareeb is not in my parent's flat. He never was.

I leave and return to the stairs. Emerging onto the building's roof, the first thing I see is the curling foam at the tops of the waves. In the bright moonlight, it looks like the sea is splitting apart and spilling its innards.

Then I see Al Ghareeb. He is standing by the elevator motor room, arms crossed over his chest, examining something.

I stand next to him. He is gazing at a mural that stretches across one of the motor room's walls.

'This is the end,' he says.

We look at the marks of paint that fill the wall from end to end. It is all yellow, every stroke of it in bright shades that are like the ringing of a bell. Unlike all the other murals, there are no figures here and no scenes of the past. It is an abstract profusion of shapes that remake the wall into a volume of brilliant light.

'Did you bring your knife?' he asks.

'No.'

'Do you like the mural?'

'I do.'

'Do you know what it is?'

'No. It's not like any of the others.'

'It's what comes after.'

'After what?'

'After tonight.'

'Tonight is the end.'

'Yes,' he nods. 'And this is what comes after.'

We are quiet for some time, as the fireworks and the ocean work themselves into a frenzy above and below us.

Then Al Ghareeb says he wants to ask me a question.

'All this time,' he says, 'have you been running from me? Or running toward me?'

'Does it matter?'

'Not really. All streets lead to the same sea.'

Standing here together, looking at this mural that makes no sense, I feel the pulse in the burn on my jaw slow and then fade. The tide is beginning to change.

'You can't hurt anyone else,' I say. 'I can't let you.'

'Who have I hurt?'

'I've seen what you can do. What you did to Conestoga.'

'I didn't do anything to Caleb.'

In the sky, the fireworks are reaching their furious midnight conclusion, with every moment bringing another boom of color that rains down toward the earth. In the space between two explosions, I begin to speak. There is something I want to explain to Al Ghareeb, because I know now that he has been walking for so long. Still watching the mural, I tell him how the sea taught me the truth about time. About how there was only ever now, this present moment in which anything can happen.

'The night you were created,' I continue, 'I stared at the sea for so long that I understood that it in itself *was* time. In a way, it was everything that had ever been done to me. The sea was roaring proof.'

It did not just apply to the future, I said, not just to the ever-increasing entropy we are always surging toward, it applied also to the past. It had worked its way backward and forward through my life, shining caustic light into every shadow. Everything was irradiated with clarity. Green plastic spoons and clocks keeping different times, the lock on my bedroom door and the cold silence that lasted for years. The way my parents were wrong about everything, but most of all themselves. With the sea I understood that every single day was every permutation folded in on itself; I was an empty street that ended exactly where it began.

When I finish speaking, I turn to face Al Ghareeb. For the first time I see that he looks young. Fragile and young. Not an abomination from the bottom of the sea who clatters the streets and terrorizes the world, but a lost and aching lonely thing. I was never meant to be frightened of him at all. He was there at the side of the road in the desert and he was there in the bathroom beneath the falling missiles and now he is here at the top of this building with the sea at his back and what comes after glowing before him.

'It's alright,' I say. 'You can go now.'

In his eyes, relief. An untethering.

Overhead there comes a climax of noise, a cavalcade of lights and patterns – it is the finale of the fireworks. They tear through the sky and rip apart the stars and, when I tip my head back to look up at them, I see something that I recognize. There, in the shuddering luminosity, is the crack in the world that I saw when I was standing on the curb just before my accident. It is a crack spilling forth a filament of pure light, and I am reaching with my hands now to my chest and my stomach, to my throat and my face, trying to find the place where I was once split open, the place through which poured the whole world. All this time I thought there was nothing, that I was nothing, and now, to see it revealed like this, to be shown the glowing center resplendent with meaning, I can only let myself fill with its promise.

Beside me, Al Ghareeb takes a breath and then lets it go. The gathered-up air of the storm, the deep secret reaches of the sea, all of it pours out. At the bottom of his exhale, there is a moment of equilibrium – a time when we are not two, but one. We have been here together on this roof above the sea for so long.

I turn back to the mural as Al Ghareeb goes. I can hear every one of his steps, a sharp rattle that softens as he leaves me behind. I trace the lines of the painting with my eyes, the way the strokes drop toward the base of the wall before launching themselves upward, like the volley and sink of a heartbeat. The yellow is familiar, and I realize I have seen it before. It is the same shade that flowed through one of the two doors facing the man in the mural by the water chamber. While one door led to the cold menace of the stars, the other door led on to this crush of radiance.

The light of this new day is growing now, the sun bleeding over the edge of the world, spilling across the sea. The sun – the rising sun – how long it has been since I have seen it. How long it has been since I believed it was even a possibility. Shadows are falling away, the darkness dying back, and I watch the yellow curtain of daylight swell. Overhead, the blur and mess of yesterday's shamal has faded and the sky is ripe with the promise of blue. How precious and strange is this world that did not, after all, come to an end. I think of Malak's apocalypse and wonder where in the world she is, and what she thinks of this unexpected tomorrow.

When I pull myself up onto the low wall of the building's edge and stand there in the wind with the sea laid out before me, I remember standing in the water chamber, seeing the gleam of its shallow puddle. How my body had swayed forward. Looking out at the endless blue dream of water below me now I am thinking of nothing and then I am thinking of everything. There is still the fear – that has not changed. Now, though, it is not the only thing here with me. There are now doorways and alleys and visions of more to come: there will be a tomorrow and I will see it.

I jump.

All of everything falls with me. This fall has been going on for some time and I recognize the rhythms. In my blood and in my bones and in the scalded skin of my body there is only the glorious yellow crescendo of this moment, this soaring, helpless ascent. There is a light so clear that it shows me the wide-open sweep of the world, the pale palm of the sky, and the generous lap of the waiting sea. I rise upward into it.

Acknowledgements

I would like to thank:

Vicki Heath Silk for her keen eye and the brilliant cover.
Cody, for everything.

About the author

Natasha Burge is a Saudi-born American writer whose family lived in the Arabian Gulf for more than half a century. She holds a PhD in creative writing and her work has been published around the world, anthologized, nominated for a Pushcart Prize, made a finalist for the Restless Books Prize for New Immigrant Writing and the Dzanc Books Prize for Fiction, and translated into Arabic, Mandarin, and Japanese.

Made in the USA
Middletown, DE
21 May 2024

54478566R00144